The Broken Lute

The Broken Lute

Ruth Berman

FTL Publications
Minneapolis, Minnesota

FTL Publications
P O Box 22693
Minneapolis, MN 55422-0693
www.ftlpublications.com
mail@ftlpublications.com

Cover art by GetCovers

Printed in the United States of America

ISBN 978-1-936881-90-1

Table of Contents

Dedication

"The Broken Lute" grew out of a dream I had one night that seemed to me, when I woke, the end of a story. I wanted to try starting in on writing the start of the story—but I was at a science-fiction convention, and hadn't brought any paper along. The late Bruce Pelz came to my rescue with a good-sized chunk of lined paper. So the at-last-finished story is dedicated, with gratitude, to Bruce.

Ruth

Chapter 1

Broken

As Garis flung rushes on the throne room floor, his thoughts focused on his plans to retake the kingship. The throne room should be his, as his father was the king of Emmering before the usurper Dale. Now, he was only a servant at the castle, but not for long, he hoped.

He flung more rushes on the throne-room floor. The bare planks shone after their scrubbing, but a faint odor of dirt still rose from them—dirt, dung, sweat, bits of food that humans or dogs had let fall, all the signs that the castle would be the better for a good airing.

But it was the royal castle of the land of Emmering, as Dale's other castles were not, and the king was more the king in the king's castle. Servants were not expected to grumble at smells, and if the king could stand it, so could the court. Time enough to descend on another of his houses when Summer came in his strength. The king and court would be off, and the servants not in their train would have a frenzy of full castle-cleaning.

Rushes would hold the odors down well enough in the meantime. It was dull work, and Garis shivered a little in the chill of early spring. It was twenty years since Dale, the lord of Norcote, had usurped the throne of Emmering from Garis the elder. The younger had been a servant in the castle for two years.

He shook his head when he came near the dais. The throne was painted bright scarlet and gilded with lines of gold. The intricate carving of the wood underneath could hardly be seen through the layers of color.

"Gaudy nonsense," he muttered.

"Yes," said a voice behind him.

Garis's head jerked up. He turned slowly and saw a short, stocky man dressed in tunic and stockings of nondescript greyish brown, about the same color as his hair and beard. "Good morning, Juggler. Did you say something?" Garis asked politely.

Juggler grinned at him, looking like a frog, with the wide mouth stretched out on the small face. "Yes, that taste for the barbaric will overthrow my lord Norcote one day or other."

Garis stared. Juggler had been at the castle longer than Garis, but he spoke with a slight, unfamiliar accent. He was not from Emmering or the other kingdoms that bordered the Longwater, but he had a knack for the sounds of the ways people spoke and could soon speak like someone who had lived among them a long time, although he did not manage to sound like someone born to it. When asked where he came from, he would smile and answer "Far away." And when asked if he might want to go home someday, he'd think a moment and shake his head, adding, "I lost the way—and I like wandering."

As a combination of jester, minstrel, and all-purpose drudge, he was a step above Garis, who was an all-purpose drudge. He was pleasant enough to all the servants, but usually he kept his thoughts to himself.

"Shouldn't say that," said Garis.

"Gaudy? Barbaric?" said Juggler. "No law says you have to like bright colors, last I heard." He smoothed down the edge of his tunic with a self-satisfied air, as if drab were a costly dye, brushed back an imaginary feather in an imaginary cap, drew attention to a hole beginning over one elbow as if he had slashed the fabric himself and lined it with silk or cloth-of-gold, and twitched an imaginary cape to flare about him.

Garis chuckled. "That's as may be, but I don't think his majesty the king would approve of what you said, in quite the way you said it, if he'd heard you," Garis said, drawling the syllables of the title.

"Oh, I suppose he might chop off my head, if someone told tales. Yours, too, if he heard that tone of voice. What of it?"

Garis considered his grinning face. "We're even, then. Let me keep my head, and you can keep yours." He turned away with another armload of rushes and began dropping them.

Juggler swayed forward. It could almost have been a bow. "Thank you, Sire."

Garis swung round, dropping the bundle of rushes. "What did you—"

A trumpet blared in the hallway.

Garis grunted in exasperation, kicked the rushes to cover as much of the remaining bare floor as possible, and withdrew to a corner, where he knelt. There was no time to get out of the room. Finishing the floor—and his question to Juggler—would have to wait until after the trial sessions.

King Dale walked briskly into the room, glittering in his green state robe with the golden heads of wheat sewn on it. After him came his son Lyndred, and the newcomer to the court, his niece Dianor, and a train of courtiers, secretaries, plaintiffs, defendants, guardsmen, and captives after them. Most of the time would go to plaintiffs and defendants and their arguments with each other. There were not many captives, and not many charges of treason among them. But there were still a few each.

Dale was not popular, but he had held the throne a long time and felt secure enough to dismiss some charges. He put the remaining offenders up for auction as forced labor to nobles who needed field workers.

Overall, Dale was as merciful a judge as he thought he could safely be, and he was considered a fair one, besides. He made a good income out of the civil cases. Most of his measures to get money were disliked, but people tangled in a dispute willingly paid to have Dale judge between them, rather than go to a local squire, who might find both sides in the wrong and settle the case more to his own advantage than to either of theirs.

Courtiers did not have to attend Dale's courts of law, in theory, but most of them thought it a good idea to be seen there, anyway. Some of them were students of law, hoping for appointments as Dale's representatives, and a smattering of law was useful no matter what kind of employment a courtier was hoping to be graced by. And the ones who were at court as hostages for their families' good behavior could not stay away too often without looking suspicious.

The trials dragged on. Dale had the patience to listen to other people's quarrels without growing noticeably bored, but yawns and smothered coughing showed that not all the court took as much interest as the king.

All at once, the trials took their attention again. Prince Lyndred stepped down from his seat on the dais and stood before the throne. "I am Lyndred, son of Dale. King, I want justice."

The idle shuffling stopped abruptly as eyes went wide, and daydreamers lost track of their dreams.

"Who has harmed you?"

"He is called Juggler. He lives in the castle."

"Let him be sent for," said Dale, but he saw Juggler in the room and waved to the crier to remain silent. He beckoned Juggler forward, omitting the ritual of searching him out.

"I'm Juggler," said Juggler. He did not look surprised at being called.

"Go on, Lyndred," said the king.

"He tried to kill me!"

The king, with a startled look at Juggler, said, "That's a serious charge."

"Lute lessons," said Lyndred bitterly. "He hit me over the head with it—just ask him."

The courtiers were mostly shocked, or managed to look as if they were but the king coughed and put his hand over his mouth and was silent for a moment. Some of the captives giggled, but the king looked at them, and they stopped.

"Well, Juggler," said the king, "Lyndred charges murder. What is your answer?"

Juggler spread his hands wide. "Your majesty, Prince Lyndred has not mentioned that he played a certain number of wrong notes in his lesson. It is the custom among many teachers to chastise students to help them remember. Perhaps it is not a wise custom. I fear that I misjudged the force of —" He hesitated, and stopped for a moment. Pomposity amused Dale sometimes, but it also alerted him to the likelihood that someone was trying to bamboozle him. A muscle twitched at the corner of the king's mouth, but it looked more like annoyance than laughter. Juggler started again. "I didn't mean to hurt him."

Dale considered that a moment and looked questioningly at the prince.

"Oh, he meant it," said Lyndred. "You don't stun with a blow without meaning it. It's no thanks to you I'm awake and seeing straight. And the lute's broken—cracked right up the curve."

"I can mend it. And you're awake and seeing straight. Prince, I lost my temper. I'm sorry."

"And you meant *no* harm?" said the king, skeptically.

"No, that is—well—" He trailed off and gave up.

"And you think he meant murder, Lyndred?" said the king.

Lyndred scowled. "No," he said at last.

"Take off your shirt," the king told Juggler, and turned to his son. "Hit him five times with the flat of the sword, and let that be an end of it."

Two guards took hold of Juggler's arms.

The prince carried out the sentence with precision. The edge of the sword did not even scratch the skin, but the crisscrossed outlines of five blades stood out in raised red patches on Juggler's back. He gave a yell at each blow, and when the guards let him go, he sagged to his knees.

The king said, "Juggler, I don't want you to misjudge your force again—or judge it, either. Put yourself among the teachers who do not chastise their students. You may continue the lessons."

"But the lute—" said the prince.

"When will it be mended?" The king waited patiently while Juggler wiped his eyes, struggled to his feet again, and eased his shirt on gingerly.

"I'm not sure how long it will take, your majesty." Teacher and student looked hopefully at the king.

"See to it that it's not too long." The king rose, annoyed with both of them. "Take the condemned to the dungeons. The king will judge no more today."

"Way for the king!" said the crier.

King and court went out with trumpets.

Garis waited for the door to close after them before he moved. Juggler was beginning to sway on his feet. Garis took his arm, steadying him gently. "I see why you took a dislike to our royal family so suddenly." He helped him sit down on the step of the dais.

Juggler, instead of answering Garis directly, looked at the door. "Your majesty," he said to the door, "Would you like a better defense? I couldn't have hurt him. His head's made of wood—good, solid oak. I was only punishing the lute for leading his fingers to the wrong notes. Now if we could get the lute bespelled to play only the right notes—"

Garis laughed. "I don't think even the most skilled of wizards would undertake to work out an enchantment that complicated."

"Well," said Juggler, "I thought I'd do better to suppose there was a chance I would still be alive after. But I'd almost rather I'd said what I thought if it meant I wouldn't have to go on teaching a lout of a pupil born of a hide-changing pig-fish from the mud of the low-tide flats." He might have gone on cursing his patron and his patron's family, but Garis interrupted.

"Yes, I can see why you thought it might not matter what you said. Not to you. But it could have mattered to me. Guard your tongue, Juggler."

"Even with only you to hear?" said Juggler, looking at him steadily.

Garis returned the look. "Calling a servant 'sire' is—foolish."

"Is that what it is?" Juggler said. Garis was still too young to have a full beard, and he went shaven rather than grow a patchy one. His face was round and wide, with brown eyes set a little too close together. His eyebrows were almost the same color as his eyes, a little darker than the hair on his head. His beard, if he had grown it, would have been streaked with light and darker browns, Juggler felt sure. "There's more than one kind of folly, boy. I know old Garis's infant son was supposed to have died of the plague, but I can't be the only one who's noticed that you look like paintings of the old king."

"That's not so uncommon. The family's been in the kingdom a long time."

"Yes?" said Juggler. "I haven't noticed any of the like with a name the like of yours. What possessed you to come here under your own name?"

"I answer to it quickly. And anyway, the name's common enough."

"Oh! Well—yes, I suppose so. But why come at all? Castle-cleaning may bring you near the throne, but it doesn't give you the power to sit on it."

Garis sat down beside him on the step and propped his head on his hands, then twisted it sideways for another look at Juggler. "Can I trust you?"

"If you have to ask—no, certainly not."

"Sorry." Garis thought some more.

The loss of temper that had led Juggler to trial made his feelings clear enough, and now the process of being tried, even though the king had treated him leniently, had made him all the angrier. And Dale would not be likely to forget the incident.

"I could use a minstrel. Will you enter my service?"

"What's the pay?"

"Dreams and a promise."

Juggler smiled. "Long time since I worked for that. Doesn't go far on an empty stomach, but my stomach's full at the moment. What will you have, a song on the line of Norcote? It's an epic theme—and I know just the epic." The epic in question was, evidently, not one of the most dignified. Juggler glanced at the gilding on the throne, and at the pile of old rushes. "Already I feel the breath of Song—"

"You'd better not feel it here," said Garis. "Meet me at the dungeon stairs at midnight. You could have your song ready for us then, if you like."

"Us? You mean you have a working conspiracy, youngster? You may sit on that throne yet."

"Yes." Garis picked up his load of dirty rushes. "Till midnight."

Juggler started to answer, but the great door opened. Half expecting an armed guard to enter, it took him a moment to focus down on the girl who stood hesitating at the threshold. "Why, Bramble, you startled me. Did you come about your stilt? Yes, I finished mending it. I have it ready for you, if you can wait a moment while I go and get it."

"Oh, thanks, Juggler!" said the girl. She was the head cook's daughter, and regularly broke into hives when made to help in the kitchen, which was, said her parents, an affliction and a trial. She served instead as a message and errand runner, and delighted in any excuse—even hives—to run, jump, or climb. "Yes, please—I mean—no," she said, brushing the tangle of straight reddish hair out of her eyes. "I was sent to tell you the king wants you to attend him in his chambers."

Juggler scratched his beard and touched the bare skin at the throat beneath it. "Thank you, Bramble. I'll get your stilt to you after supper, then." He looked sideways at Garis. "I hope," he said, and hurried from the room.

Behind him, Garis followed, rush-laden, and Bramble trotted along beside him to hold the doors on the way to the midden.

Juggler found the king, and the prince as well, glaring at one another.

The king had put off his formal robe and looked colorless in the plain undergown of undyed white wool, but he sat as erect on the edge of his bed as if it had been the throne of judgment. The prince still wore his particolor tunic of white and blue. The little motions of hands and arms, or legs when he shifted his weight, were exaggerated by the contrast of the colors, and he looked like the river-waves his garb meant.

"Your majesty?" Juggler bowed courteously, and waited.

"Have you finished the song Prince Lyndred is writing to the lady Dianor?" The king did not bother to look at Juggler, but went on considering Lyndred thoughtfully.

Lyndred straightened proudly under the inspection.

"Yes, your—" Juggler started.

"Why do I have to bother with that nonsense?" said Lyndred.

"You want to be king after me, don't you?"

"Who wouldn't?" said the prince lightly, but his father did not smile.

"That, my boy, is precisely the point." Dale wrapped the woolen undergown more closely around himself. "Your cousin is descended from the kings. Her grandmother was Berlik's daughter. That's long ago now, but there it is. Any man who married her would have a claim to the throne, and a better claim than I have."

The prince laughed. "You *have* the throne." He gathered several stray cushions together into a heap, and after glancing at his father for permission, dropped down onto it. He tucked his legs in close and wrapped his arms around his knees.

The king said quietly, "Yes, I have the throne. I could have a civil war, too—or you could—if someone else marries Lady Dianor."

"Yes, but she knows that. We were friends when we were youngsters, so far as I remember. Tell her to marry me! She'd be willing enough—she wouldn't want a war."

The king shook his head. "Don't give orders when you can persuade. Especially don't give orders to a noble with powerful friends. They might think a war would be worth it. They have power, and they wouldn't mind more."

"Let them try—I'd like to see them," said Lyndred defiantly.

"I wouldn't." The king tugged at his beard for a moment. "And I don't think it will take an unreasonable amount of what you call nonsense to woo her. You're likeable enough, when you put your mind to it. Juggler, let's have the song."

Juggler looked out the window into the strip of blue beyond the wall and above the forest, and sang.

> You are the daystar, my delight.
> You are the dawning of my sight.
> What did I ever see before I knew
> The day you brought with you?
>
> I walk the dark and search for day,
> Lost in the shadows—out of my way.
> When the daystar brings the light
> The sky is bright.

"It'll do," said the king grudgingly. He looked at his son. "Do you know the tune?"

"Yes, it's the one I was playing."

Juggler tensed, expecting a glare, but the prince was suddenly more cheerful.

"And I can't sing it without the lute—I don't stay on key by myself." He scrambled to his feet. "Have I your leave, Father?"

"No."

The prince raised his eyebrows, but sat down again. There was no use protesting that tone of voice. He hugged his knees, settling comfortably back into the pillows.

The king turned his attention back to Juggler. "Can the lute be fixed by tonight?"

Juggler shook his head.

The king mused a little while, and then said, "After supper, Lyndred, ask Lady Dianor to come to see the new hall."

Dale had redecorated and enlarged the hall where entertainments in the castle were held, planning to win admiration with handsome images of the spirits of the seasons and handsome welcome for any who cared to come join them in the holidays of the season changes. The extra money required had not been popular, but the results were expected to be attractive enough to counteract any grumbling. "If she waits till the spring dances begin, she'll only see it covered with people, after all. And as for what the new tiles cost to show the gods of the seasons in their splendor, I'd be glad to have someone who'll like them to admire them now. Juggler, you will happen to be at the organ when they arrive, and able to play a tune, if the prince should happen to ask for one."

Juggler opened his mouth but turned the sound that came out into a cough and said nothing.

The king looked at him quizzically.

"It won't sound the way it should on the organ," said Juggler slowly. "It ought to have a lighter tone."

The king looked out the window. "I know. But some music my son must have, and floor tiles can't sing. If you can't fix the lute—then it's the organ."

"Yes, your majesty."

"Make sure Lyndred has a copy of the words to memorize." He glanced at his son. "And memorize them."

"Yes, Father." Lyndred said, accepting the necessity—and the piece of paper Jugger slid out of his pocket and offered him.

The king turned back from the window and leaned over to pat Lyndred's shoulder. "Now you have leave," he said.

Lyndred climbed to his feet, stretched thoroughly, and made his bow.

As the permission to go away obviously included them both, Juggler opened the door for the prince, made his own bow to the king, and followed Lyndred out.

At sunset Juggler ate his supper hurriedly and slipped out of the servants' hall through the kitchen. There he caught Bramble, returning with empty bottles, and asked the girl to work the bellows for him. He waited while Bramble went out again with beer for the pages to serve the court. Juggler peeped into the long room where tables were set. The prince and Dianor were still in place. She was dressed simply, in a red gown and lighter red undergown, with none of the embroidery of cloud and acorn that belonged to her father's family, or the wheat of the kings. Sweets were going round. The meal was almost over.

Juggler hurried away with Bramble to the ritual-hall. They lit the tapers by the door and the organ. The statues of the gods in the corners were just visible in the shadows: the green Spring maid with her bowl of water, the red Field king with his torch, the gold Harvest mother, her feet covered with earth, and a loaf of bread in her hands, and the Winter father with his silver cape blown back in the wind.

The tiles at their bases repeated their images, as if they stood over mirrors, or beside still lakes.

Bramble went behind him to the bellows, and Juggler plopped himself down on the stool in front of the organ. He played a few of the rolling chords from a harvest song and worried over it. The organ could drown out a sweet nothing with a single note. Touching the keys as lightly as he could, he played his daystar song on the topmost octaves of the keyboard. Even the higher tones were too massive for the lilting tune, but it would have to do. He waited patiently, thinking of songs, and it was not long before he heard laughter in the corridor outside, like an echo to the music.

Dianor came through the arch, and the prince after her, saying, "What's the joke?"

"Nothing," said Dianor, and laughed again.

Lyndred gave her a questioning look.

She waved her hands in a gesture of apology. "I just remembered how you used to hate dancing and ceremonies when we were little. And to think of your offering to walk in here when you didn't have to!"

The prince was disconcerted. He tried to think of an appropriate reply, but could not find one. Instead, he jumped to his rehearsed comment. "I had a song to welcome you home, Cousin. Would you like to hear it?"

"Yes," said Dianor, looking startled. She turned away from the statue of the Winter father, which she had been comparing to the tiled Winter stretching out from the statue's base. "Thank you."

He swallowed, made a bow for luck to the Spring maid, then took a deep breath and nodded to Juggler, who began to play.

Lyndred sang the song creditably, after all, even if he squeaked on the high notes from trying not to shout them. He had a clear, pleasant voice, in spite of his hatred of lessons for it.

Dianor was duly impressed with the compliment. "Oh, Lyndred, I like that," she said. "And you wrote it?"

"No," he said, truthfully, and decided that wasn't courteous. "The minstrel helped," he added. He held out a hand to Juggler in token of the contribution.

"Thank you," she said, hesitating, because she did not know what to call him.

"I'm Juggler," he said.

She looked him over, working diligently at the task of learning to match people to labels. It did not seem to occur to her to care that his rank was such that she did not have to bother.

Lyndred cleared his throat, impatient with her attention to the player. "I spend most of my time on patrol with the guard, you know," he put in, by way of elaboration. "Especially since the raids back and forth with King Wyrond in Melibos began."

Dianor nodded gravely. "Pity he's so greedy. If he hadn't raided us when—"

"Well, we went in first," said Lyndred.

"What? But—why?"

"He would've been first if we hadn't."

Dianor looked doubtful.

"You don't understand, Cousin," said Lyndred earnestly. "Think of all the kingdoms here in the north. How many can you name that are at peace with all their neighbors?"

"Several." She bent her head, concentrating on the pattern of green and gold, red and silver in the floor tiles as she tried to find the names. The complicated curves twined themselves across the full length of the floor, only taking identifiable shapes where they turned into gods in the corners.

"There are some," said the prince, seating himself on a bench by the wall. "Poor ones, or hidden in the mountains."

Dianor shook her head and sat down beside him. "I think you're wrong."

He took her hand. "Well, it's the Spring maid who rules when peace comes, so I suppose women aren't really supposed to understand war."

She frowned, ready to argue this point, but he went on.

"In your situation, though, you ought to."

"What do you mean?"

"Well, if you wanted to, you could make a claim to the throne, you know."

"I don't want to."

"Anyone who married you would have a claim to the throne. There'd be two claimants, two factions, and a war between them if someone else married you. So I have to."

"You have to! Not if I know it!" She pulled her hand free and jumped up, then stood speechless, trying to think of something nasty enough to do herself justice. If she had had a weapon to hand—even if it were no more than a lute—she might have followed Juggler's example and tried to express her feelings by making an assault on her cousin.

Juggler froze into silence. He would have liked to warn Bramble to keep still as well, but he could not make a signal without drawing attention he did not want to attract under the circumstances. But no doubt Bramble would be quick enough to understand that quarreling nobles did not appreciate distractions.

"I didn't mean it the way it sounded," said the prince. He tried to frame a defense, an apology, and a change of subject all in one, and sat stuttering. His father, stopping to look in on them as he went to his chambers, gave him an excuse to abandon the attempt. "Here's Father to talk to you," the prince said. "Shall I tell your waiting-women to be ready to attend you?" He left without waiting for an answer.

"Dianor," said the king, "what's the matter, child?"

She was silent, waiting for her anger to cool. Her cousin had meant well, clearly enough. He might jerk his hands as if he hoped to shake an apology out at the fingertips instead of putting one into words properly, as he should have done, but his distress at having hurt her feelings had been plain to see. She managed a smile and sat down again. "I'm afraid we were quarreling, Uncle. Lyndred seems to think that fighting your neighbors is the most important thing he can do."

"It may not sound so, put that way," said the king, "but I think it is. It's no wonder if my son thinks so, too."

"Justice is more important."

"How very abstract youngsters can be!" he said, smiling at her.

She looked up at him from the bench where she sat, irritated at his evasion and the touch of mockery. "Yes, but it is," she said, not letting the subject drop.

"Very likely. But it takes power to defend justice, and the one who holds the power is the one who must decide what justice is—it's part of the power. Try again."

"Love is more important." She glanced up at him, and out of the corner of her eye saw Juggler, hunched over the keyboard, with his hands in his lap, trying to look as if he weren't there. "Music and art," she added.

The king said, "You look as your aunt Dianor did at your age."

"My aunt?"

The king sighed and sat down next to her. "Your father's sister. She died before you were born." Then he went back to the neglected argument. "Love and art?—pleasanter, of course. But they don't matter over time. If you do nothing but love someone, or something pretty, you're forgotten and nameless in a hundred years."

"People remember artists."

"Oh, yes." The king leaned back on the bench and pointed a finger in Juggler's direction without bothering to look at him. "The bards remain. But I'm not a bard. Short of inspiring Juggler to write an epic to glorify my reign, his immortality, if he wins it, means nothing to me. But suppose I am so wicked as to bring the red sword and conquer the northlands. With one law to govern all those little kingdoms, trade will be easier, and they won't be able to fight each other. In a hundred years, the people on the borders perhaps need not worry that their homes may be burned once in the year by raiders."

"Your raiders," said Dianor stubbornly.

"And my neighbors' raiders. The nobles will not send people and grain to the wars, and the people will be glad not to be sent." He mused for a moment, looking about the hall. "I don't suppose the grain will care," he added lightly, then shrugged, and said, "Lovers won't care, either, but lovers in the first glory of finding one another have never had eyes to spare to watch how the world wags."

Dianor stood up. "I never knew I had an aunt."

"It was many years ago, child."

"Were you in love with her, Uncle?"

"Yes."

She bent and kissed his forehead. "Good night," she said, and left him.

He sat where he was, apparently remembering another Dianor, one who had left him and married the king whose crown and throne had been seized by Dale. At last he got up and stood in the hall a moment, looking at the reflections of flames glinting on the Winterfather's cape, the one on the statue and the one in the tiles below it. Then he snuffed out the tapers by the door and left.

Juggler let out his breath with a gasp. He might be an immortal bard by the king's account, but he didn't think it was healthy to have overheard so much. Either the king had then forgotten he was there, or didn't think he mattered. Whichever it was, he hoped his majesty would continue of the same mind. His head ached with holding so still and trying not to breathe noticeably. "Come out, Bramble," he said.

The girl crept out from behind the organ and looked up at him as if wanting to ask questions.

Juggler smiled, and shook his head.

Bramble opened her mouth, closed it, thought, and then said only, "I liked the song."

"Thanks." Juggler turned away and snuffed the remaining tapers, beside the organ. They blundered through the darkness to the archway, and went silently to the servants' quarters. Their only conversation was a subdued, "Thank you," from Bramble, when Juggler gave her back the mended stilt.

Bramble went on to her parents' room, holding the wooden stave delicately, as if she put no faith in splints and glue. And so much the better, Juggler thought, if it made her more careful when she tried it again. Youngsters who broke stilts could just as well break their legs.

Juggler dropped down on the pallet.

He meant only to rest, in case he slept past midnight, when he was to meet Garis. But other servants were going to sleep around him, and his eyes closed.

Chapter 2
Dungeon and Manor

Juggler woke in a panic, sure that he had slept through to dawn. Looking about, he saw a candle still burning. The servants were not supposed to waste good wax, or even tallow, but between carelessness and fear of the dark, the sleeping quarters stayed lit sometimes, more often than the steward liked.

Juggler guessed the time was near midnight. He could tell he had been dreaming, although the dream had vanished out of reach as he woke, leaving only a sense of walking, but he could not tell where or why. He did not have the feeling of a long string of dreams behind the one he had lost, so the night could not possibly be gone, even if he had not had the evidence of the candle. He rubbed the rheum from his eyes and sat up. His back had almost stopped hurting.

He felt his way through darkness and shadows to the head of the dungeon stairs. As he crouched there, the bell began its count. It was just midnight.

The door at the foot of the stairs was open. A large young jailer was sitting quietly sewing a patch on the elbow of his tunic.

"Good evening, Juggler," said a low voice behind him.

"Garis?"

"Yes." Garis brushed past him and started down.

"Wait, the jailer—"

"Don't worry. He's on our side."

"Oh," said Juggler thoughtfully.

The jailer put down his sewing and took his knife out of the sheath, but when he could make out their faces he grinned and put the knife back. He looked at Juggler, and then questioningly at Garis, who nodded. He sat back to make room for them to go by.

"Evening, Dikon. Can we go out now?"

"Yes. The jail-master went to bed an hour ago." Dikon mimed a tottering step of aged weariness. It looked odd on his wide, healthy frame. "Going to be a meeting? Some went out poaching, and some couples went out to be alone."

"Yes, I want a meeting," said Garis, "but near dawn will do well enough for it."

"Going to tell our friend outside?" said Dikon.

Juggler blinked approvingly at the cautious namelessness of Dikon's reference.

Garis grinned for a moment, taking note of Juggler's approval, and told Dikon, "I'll tell her, but I won't be asking her to send anyone to attend. Too risky."

Dikon took the great-key to the inner door, which he opened for them. It creaked. Beyond was a hallway with dirty iron doors along each side, and whips and rods hanging neatly over the doors.

"Pretty," said Juggler.

Garis scowled. "Isn't there any fat or oil to rub on the hinges? That creaking could draw attention."

"Jail-master won't let us put any on. Says it's a saving to our lord the king if we wait until the doors as good as won't open. Myself, I think he likes the noise. Reminds him he's in charge." Dikon pulled himself up to his full height, and cast a haughty glare around the little domain, then made a face and locked the doors after them. "Cell doors're all open."

Garis entered the nearest cell, pulled the bars out of its little window, and leaned them against the wall.

Juggler gave a startled look at the little open square. "Can you get out of all the cells like that?"

"The ones that have windows."

"In other words, not many?"

"Not many," Garis agreed. "We've cut tunnels to connect to them from a few of the rest, but it takes a long time. I'd like more, but we manage, more or less. And we don't want to risk a cave-in—too much commotion, and our little rat-holes would get stopped up."

From outside the cell, Dikon said, "Large rats, I think."

Garis laughed. He jumped up, pulled himself through, and scrambled out to the air. Juggler, grunting as he pulled himself up, because the strain pulled on his sore back, followed after. At the top, he found himself on grass between the castle wall and a privet bush. It was budding, and scratchy for two people to be squeezed behind.

"What do you have your conspiracy doing, then, if tunnels are out?" he asked, as Garis squeezed back down and reached into the cell to grab the bars and pull them back into place.

"Poaching in the woods takes a good deal of the night-time. His majesty's vitaillers don't allot much to the dungeons, and we want them better fed than that."

"They're going to be your army?" Juggler asked.

"Part of it," Garis said. "Some get taken to work as forced labor on large estates, and—" He stopped, wary of naming names. "Some of the owners will support me."

Juggler looked at him doubtfully. "Forced labor usually means working in the fields, doesn't it? Do you really think they can be forced to fight?"

"Not all. Probably some. It's not as if they have much reason to want Dale kept in charge in Emmering," Garis peered into the darkness beyond the privet. There were no watchers happening by. He bent low and raced across the grass, Juggler following close behind him, into the shelter of a clump of rosebushes in tubs. The gardener was taking a chance, putting them out so early in the year. A freezing cold night would be the end of the blooms that had opened while the bushes were still indoors. The dew on the leaves glistened in the light of the moon, just visible over the wall of the castle grounds. The red of the flowers was invisible. They looked black, and the rose smell coming from them seemed unlikely. Beyond were more bushes, some budding, and some coming into leaf, then a space of clear grass, and finally the wall. Garis stopped in the cover of a lilac. "Mind your footing," he said.

"What footing?"

Garis touched something that looked like a bit of moss or lichen growing.

Juggler bent close to it, but it still didn't look like anything. He put out his hand to touch it. It was the head of a spike, driven into the wall, so far that only a bit of the end stuck out.

"There's space to stand and space to grab," said Garis, "but be careful. Most the lichens are only lichens, and the moss won't hold you."

Juggler clicked his tongue doubtfully. More exercise on a sore back.

Garis set off up the spiked wall, and Juggler followed him. It was easier than the scramble out of the tiny window, but harder on his nerves, because of the possibility that a guard with particularly good night vision might catch sight of shadows moving where they should not.

Another column of licheny spikes took them down the outside of the wall.

They stood in the ditch of the wall in the great park which separated the castle from the village on one side, and from the forest, the rest of the way round. Juggler pointed toward the village, as a question.

"No," Garis whispered. "This way." He set off at a run, sticking close to the wall. There were watchtowers above them at intervals, but the wall itself hid them from any guards above. Watching and listening for any stray guards on the ground, they followed the turn of the wall until they were on the far side from the village, with forest across the clearing from them. They waited for a cloud to hide the moon, then bent themselves double and scuttled over the open ground into the trees.

When they were well hidden by forest, Juggler said, "May I ask some foolish questions?"

"Why not?" said Garis.

"Why are you even alive? The queen was about to have a child, by what I've heard, but when Dale killed the king and queen— "

"He put about the story that they were both killed that night. But in the darkness and confusion the queen—" Garis stopped and changed his choice of a word for one he had not grown up able to use much. "My mother managed to get out of the castle grounds and escape through the woods to—to a supporter. She went into labor there and died in the birthing. There'd been a stillborn child on the estate recently, and my mother was buried by the body. When Dale went looking for news of what had become of them he was shown the bodies. There was a cousin who'd married a noble across the river in Melibos, and I was smuggled out—in a load of wheat, I'm told—and I was raised in Melibos." He hesitated, considered, then sighed, and said,

"I'm sometimes not so sure that I'm feeling that I ought to have Emmering to give a peaceful reign to the people here as it is that I want to protect the people in Melibos from the war that will come when Dale feels his strength is enough to let him conquer them. I grew up with them, and they know well enough that he thinks their land would be a tempting target."

Juggler considered this strategy and said at last, "Then what are you waiting for? I can see you're using the trials to conscript an army for yourself—"

"Dale has a fairly large army of his own, you may have noticed," said Garis.

Juggler waved this consideration aside. "—but suppose you just killed the king and prince one day and proclaimed yourself the true king. What could anyone do about it?"

"Refuse to believe it," said Garis. "Have you spoken much with the guardsmen?"

"Not much."

"They're like ivy." Garis stopped to touch the bole of a great oak. The vine-leaves were only just coming out, but the stems grew so thickly that he had to shove hard to get at the bark. "Sooner or later the oak will be smothered."

"I don't follow." The night air was cold now that they had stopped, and Juggler shivered. The grass was too wet to sit on, so he stood quietly, hands dangling. He was not out of breath, but the feeling of danger from getting out of the dungeon and off the castle grounds without the formality of an open gate seemed to have a similar effect on his throat. Even with the chill in the air, he was glad enough to be at rest for a moment.

Garis leaned against the oak, idly picking off tendrils as he spoke. "Anyone can take the throne—anyone's right to it is as good as King Dale's. Lord Norcote needed a strong army to win the throne and to keep him there as king, but now he has to keep them busy, or one of them might follow his example. Wars keep the soldiers busy and win them enough glory to keep their minds off the throne. He has to keep fighting, and by fighting he trains more soldiers who have to be kept busy."

"I don't think he sees it that way," said Juggler.

"I don't know about that," said Garis. "But what I see—I see that if I don't overthrow the king, one of his captains will, some day or other." He wiped his hands off on the open patch of oak-bark he had produced. "If I do it, and do it with some force to back me, not just an attack on Dale by myself, they'll hesitate before trying it—at least, once I've managed to hold on a while. Some'll be bound to try at first. They'll have two good examples to follow." He brushed some bits of moss and tendril off the front of his tunic. "Come on—any guests should be gone or asleep by now."

"Gone from where?" said Juggler, running to catch up.

"My chief councilor, you might say."

The wood came to an end abruptly, against a line of high, thick blackthorn hedge, too thick to see through. It went a long way off on both sides. In one direction, Juggler could not make out anything, but in the other the hedge apparently turned a corner, and he caught a glimpse of open space in the moonlight. He blinked as his world, turned about by the rambling way they had taken through the forest, suddenly oriented itself. The open space was a bit of the road to the south, and they were outside the holdings of Lady Eldwin. She was said to be wealthy and eccentric, loving solitude, and rarely came to court. It was a useful reputation for a surviving noble from the reign of King Dale's predecessor.

Garis turned right, away from the road, and followed the hedge a few yards, then stooped and pushed aside a group of branches near the ground—carefully, because of the thorns— revealing a hole, half cut through the hedge and half dug beneath it. A squirrel, frightened by the shifting in the branches, leaped to the top of the hedge and sat there scolding them until they were safely out the other side.

On the other side was a field of what would be barley, although it had not yet been sown. Manure had been spread out and mixed with the earth, ready for the seed. They pinched their noses against the smell and ran across. Beyond it a footpath began, and led them to the manor.

Garis knocked at a side door. They scraped their shoes off on the step, and after a few moments a sleepy servant let them in, holding a candle high to see their faces. He gave a nod at sight of Garis, and turned back to him with a questioning look after he found an unfamiliar face in Juggler.

"Friend of mine," said Garis.

The door-ward let them pass, then rubbed his eyes, pulled the door to, and curled up on his bench again, leaving them to find their own way.

Juggler followed Garis into a room warmed by a good fire, although dim, because there was no other light. With heat to hand, Juggler discovered that he felt chilled through from their walk. "Sorry," he said, and brushed ahead of Garis to get closer to the fire. "Sorry," he said again, realizing that there was someone sitting on a heap of cushions there. He bowed, guessing it was the lady of the manor.

Eldwin looked up, startled at their arrival. She had been going over a book of records, but she set a marker in it, closed it, and put out her hand for Juggler to help her up. She stood, stretched, and gave Garis a smile. "Welcome," she said. She was taller than Garis, with a thin, lined face, and grey hair hanging loose from under a grey cap.

She glanced from Garis to Juggler with a questioning look.

"I'm called Juggler," he said and turned his own inquiring look to Garis. Lady Elwin was obviously the "supporter" who had given his mother refuge, but if Garis thought it safer for him not to know that for sure, he was probably right. Garis smiled, without acknowledging what he could see Juggler guessed.

"Good morning, my lady," said Garis.

"Is it so late?" Eldwin yawned, and stretched again. "I suppose it is. What's the news with you?"

Garis dropped onto another pile of cushions and tossed some of them to Juggler. "I think we may be ready to fight."

Eldwin went to a cupboard set into one wall and took out three bowls and a bottle of beer. "I agree," she said. "What changed your mind?"

"Partly him." Garis pointed a thumb at Juggler. "Juggler's a minstrel, and his songs may do something to hearten us. And I've been watching the guards train. We don't have enough fighters and weapons, but if we wait we'll be even further behind, and the longer we wait the more danger there is that we might be discovered—especially once Summer comes on the fields, and the nights will be getting short."

"Yes," said Eldwin, "though Spring's a muddy, ill-omened time for it. If you waited till Summer, or even till after the harvests ...." She clicked her tongue and fell silent. She got the bottle open and poured the beer.

Garis took a sip and swallowed. He smoothed his hands against the smoothness of the polished wood of the bowl, watching the firelight gleam against its side. He took another sip, then looked over the bowl at Eldwin and smiled at her. "What happened to my war-mongering councilor?"

Eldwin lowered herself back into her seat among the cushions by the fire. "As we come nearer to it, sire, I worry more. And you've argued all along that we need something to win spirits, aside from whatever fighting may do for us."

"It doesn't win many hearts," said Garis. He stopped for a moment, considering. "I suppose we could wait," he said doubtfully. "It's a long time till Autumn."

"And at my age," Eldwin said, "time rolls by well enough without greasing the axles."

Garis looked at Juggler. "Can you give us lucky songs?"

"Tall order," said Juggler.

"Too much for you?" said Eldwin. Her tone was joking, but Juggler recognized the question as serious. He suppressed the bragging denial that came first to mind.

"I can help," he said quietly. "But I'm no wizard."

"Brains enough to be honest," said Eldwin. She nodded to Garis, approving the new ally. "But wizardry, now that we mention it...." She fell silent again, looking into the fire. Lines of red scrawled themselves over the ashes.

"Yes?" said Garis,

"I wonder if wizardry *would* help." She turned away from the flames, blinking to try to see his face clearly, dark after the dazzle of the fire.

"No doubt it would," said Garis. "Do you have a wizard owing you a favor? Or I could go look for one with his life in danger so I could save him and be rewarded, but they don't wander around the woods catching their beards in oak stumps just for the asking."

Eldwin laughed. "No, but your father's sword was a gift of wizardcraft—did you know that?"

"Yes, but it's lost, unless Norcote has it, isn't it?"

"Certainly not." Eldwin gave a disapproving sniff. "You weren't all that your mother managed to save. She brought his sword with her, too."

"It's here?" said Garis.

"In Melibos. I thought it was safer for more dangerous charges there than here, but I thought the same place across the river there for both of you might not be the best plan. And not telling either place where the other was might be better still. All the same, Melibos for both seemed a fair plan. King Wyrond has been on unfriendly terms with Norcote, to put it at the mildest, ever since your father died, and no one had much chance to rummage through his lands for familiar-looking infants, let alone swords."

Juggler asked, "If it's a magic sword, my lady—what does it do, then?"

"*If?*" said Eldwin, and sniffed again, scornfully. Then she sighed and said ruefully, "Not enough, perhaps. Small magics are easier to come by than great ones, and not so easy as all that comes to, either. Any magic's reason enough to be grateful, and King Garis was." She glanced at the fire again and held up her hands to warm them. "Bonefrost glows when the enemy is at hand—not that you're going to be in much doubt on that score—and it's protection against poison. It chills the one you fight, and that slows some fighters down. But cold's a Winter charm, and growing weak this near to Spring."

"A winter blade?" said Garis.

"Winter's a season, too," Eldwin commented. "And you *said* you wanted something to win people's attention. Bonefrost may not be the blade you'd choose if you had the choosing, but it has the virtues it has, and it made a name for itself." She held her hands to the fire again, then wrapped her arms around her, looking puzzled. "More of a name than you might expect. Bonefrost had—and has, I believe—a reputation far beyond its known strengths, except perhaps in high Winter."

Garis leaned back against his pile of cushions. "I heard stories about Bonefrost the manslayer when I was little. Your version doesn't sound much like that." He thought a moment. "In Melibos?"

"Yes, with Hluvend."

"The wizard? Bonefrost is his work, isn't it?"

Eldwin nodded.

"Does he still live near the border?"

"So I've heard."

'Then the journey would take only a few days. But there'd be problems getting out of Emmering and into Melibos."

"Not to mention getting back out and back in again," Eldwin agreed.

Garis frowned and was silent, considering.

An idea struck Juggler just as he was about to swallow a mouthful of beer. He made a series of strange faces and managed to spit the mouthful back into his bowl before he choked. He coughed, laughed, coughed again, and got his breath under control. "Garis, I think I can get you a border-pass."

"How?" said Garis and Eldwin together.

Juggler chewed his lip, thinking the hunch through more carefully. "Well, you see, the king...." He stopped in confusion. "I don't know if this'll work. Let me try it, and if it does I'll tell you."

Eldwin frowned.

"I suppose that's asking you to take a lot on trust," said Juggler.

"It's all of that," Eldwin said wryly. "How long will it take you to find out if you've failed?" She smiled teasingly, waiting to see if he would protest against her failure-expecting choice of words.

He smiled back. "A day or so."

The question they were not asking was how they could trust Juggler not to use the time to try to win Dale's favor by telling on them. Part of the answer, no doubt, was that Garis expected to be able to keep an eye on what he did. But part of the answer seemed to be that Garis had decided he could trust Juggler— and Eldwin thought she could trust Garis's judgment.

Garis swallowed the last of his beer and set down the bowl.

Eldwin touched a finger to the bottle by way of asking if he would like another bowlful.

Garis shook his head. "We'll say good night, my lady. I'll try for Bonefrost, then, and when I get back—it'll be time."

Eldwin embraced them, and they left as silently as they had come. The servant at the door had a torch ready for them. It was colder and darker outside than it had been.

They ran, trying to keep warm, as they crossed Eldwin's land. Once in the wood they had to slow down again, but they tried to go as quickly as they could.

Juggler's head was filled by turns with schemes and rhymes. In their haste, he would have trampled straight across what looked like a patch of pale moonlight in the middle of a little clearing. Garis caught his shoulder and pulled him to a halt, glancing up and then westward.

It was not moonlight. The moon had set.

They pulled back into the trees. With the torchlight off the clearing, the "moonlight" vanished. It was a reflection off some light-colored fabric, presumably on a human wearer.

"Who's there?" It was a young woman's voice. She sounded startled rather than frightened, but she scrambled to her feet to face them—or what would have been facing them, if there'd been light enough from the torch to show their faces to each other. A glimmer in the lines of her dress showed that she had put a hand to her side, evidently prepared to draw a knife, if there was need, but her voice was calm as she said, "I went astray, I think. Can you show me the way to the castle?"

"Yes, of course," said Garis. He couldn't help adding, "You shouldn't have come out so far in darkness."

"You sound like my nurse Rosewind," she said impatiently, then contradicted herself, "No, you're right, I suppose. But I was upset, and I wanted to be alone to think, and…. But then I lost my way." She peered at them. In the wavering dimness of the torchlight it was hard to make out features. "I've seen you at the court, haven't I? Your voice sounds familiar."

"Like your nurse," Garis suggested.

She gave a snort of amusement.

Juggler frowned, recognizing the voice as Dianor's. Apparently the king's niece and the king's servant—and enemy—had each taken the other for an obscure courtier. Polite conversation was an appropriate result. He was not sure friendly conversation was.

But they were chattering, and it seemed harmless enough —what was growing, and where the roads went. To his surprise, Juggler found himself drawn into it. Dianor had never been outside Emmering, and she described to them her disappointment —childish, she called it, although she obviously still felt it—that she had come straight back to the court after her schooling and could not get permission to travel, even if it was just over the river to Melibos.

"I grew up in Melibos," Garis said.

"Is it very different?" Dianor asked.

"Not very." He added, "I used to be impatient to come to Emmering. Thought everything would be different *here*—it would be where I belonged, and everything would be easy, and...." He shrugged.

"Yes, I thought the castle would be different from school, but...." And Dianor stopped short in her turn. After a moment she added thoughtfully, "I suppose to find very different places you'd have to travel a long way."

"You could go downriver to the sea," Juggler said.

"Have you been there?" she asked.

"Sometimes you'd think he's been everywhere," said Garis. "He has good stories."

Juggler gave a cough. "Travelers have been known to exaggerate."

"Even you?" said Garis, pretending to be astonished.

Juggler grunted, by way of refusing to answer such a question, then added, "Yes, I've been down the river. The Longwater's pretty up here, blues and browns, and underneath the trees it's green, or fire colors in the Fall. Farther down, after the Stony and the Winterreach join it, it gets muddy. It's not pretty then, but it's impressive—so wide you can't see across it, some places. The current's slower, and there are lots of little islands. They keep changing over the seasons, depending on flood or drought."

Soon they drew near the wall. There they heard a whisper, carrying across the open space between the woods and the wall. "Hey, easy with that damn thing!"

Garis pulled back and turned away from the sound, leading them the long way round the wall to the main gate, not the short way, which would have passed by the ladder of spikes and whoever was near it.

Dianor looked around, trying vainly to see through the darkness. "Who's that? Thieves?" she whispered.

"Not likely," said Garis. "Poachers, I expect. They won't bother us if we stay clear."

"We should alert the guard," said Dianor.

"Not till we're in safely."

Juggler smiled to himself at Garis's tone of careful consideration. Steering Dianor away from the "poachers" was no doubt a sensible idea. What to do with her and still get all of them inside might be a problem, however. What they needed was an excuse to get her to go in alone, and an excuse for him and Garis not to need to go in with her. He tried to consult Garis, by asking, "Can we get in here? We're late—the gates must be locked."

"No, that's all right," said Dianor. "I left word with the gatesman when I came out." It had not occurred to her that her guides might not have explanations as good as hers to offer to a guard.

Garis said nothing. They could see Dianor safely inside, and consider their own standing then.

They finished the circuit of the wall, and Dianor went up to the gate. "Hello there!" she called.

"Hello," said someone sleepy. A lantern was held out over the top of the wall, dropping a pool of dim, red light around Dianor. Garis and Juggler stood back. "Oh, it's you, my lady. A moment, please."

Soon the bolts on one side of the gate clanged open. The gatesman held up his lantern again, and inspected the view. "Who's this with you, my lady?"

"I lost my way, and they led me back," she said.

Garis stepped into the light. "Good morning, Mulben. Have they stuck you with the deadwatch again?"

Juggler came forward after him, trying not to look hangdog about it.

Mulben pulled a face at Garis's question. "The captain doesn't like the way my nose twitches." It twitched as he spoke, and he scratched at it angrily. "You're out late," he added.

"We went to visit a friend and didn't notice how the time went." Garis smiled rakishly.

Mulben clicked his tongue at them. "You get fined for that, you know."

"I know," Garis said ruefully, "but there's no helping it now."

"I'll pay their fine," said Dianor.

"I'd rather you didn't, my lady," Garis began.

Juggler nudged his heel. It was not their place as servants to refuse bounty, although it was irksome to Garis to show himself now to Dianor as a servant.

Garis bent his head. "—but it's very kind of you," he finished.

Mulben bowed to Dianor and stood aside for them to enter. He held his lantern high, peering out into the darkness, to be sure there was no one else, then set the light down and put his weight to the door, swinging it back into place. He shot the bolts home again.

Dianor told Mulben about the poachers probably on the other side of the grounds, and he hurried to finish locking the bolts so that he could leave his post long enough to call out a search. He seemed to be pleased at the prospect of rousing the captain.

Dianor led the way across the grounds and into the warmth of the castle, with Garis and Juggler following respectfully.

Inside the antechamber, an old woman was sitting on a stool, dozing in the dim light of a candle. She jerked forward at the sound of the door and looked round at them, then slid off the stool. She was short, and had to jump to get her footing.

Dianor stopped, turning away from Juggler and Garis to face her.

"Well," said Rosewind grimly.

"You didn't need to wait up," said Dianor. "I left word at the gate—"

"You'll catch your death," said the nurse, gathering up a heap of cloth, which turned out to be a wool cloak. She swept it around Dianor's shoulders.

"Nurse, you shouldn't worry—"

"There's damp, there's dark, there's cold, there's beasts, there's desperate folk in the world. 'Shouldn't worry'!"

Dianor cleared her throat, ready to argue these points, but then thought better of it, and patted the older woman's shoulder. "I know, Rosewind. I'm sorry." She raised her hand to wave a quick good-night to her companions, and led her nurse away, each clearly determined to see that the other woman was robbed of no more sleep that night.

"But—" said Garis. He stopped.

"What?" said Juggler.

"Nothing. I wanted to see what she looked like." Garis looked after the nurse's retreating candle for a moment, then shook himself. "Dikon's going to get a shock when we turn up on the stairs again, instead of coming through the window like decent folk." He started toward the dungeon.

Dikon, wearing his newly-mended tunic, let them in. "What?" he said, as the quickest way of demanding an explanation.

"Some other time," said Garis. "Everyone in?"

"Yes. We have a deer cooking."

"Hunt took a long time."

Dikon nodded. "Game's getting shy."

"That's why they were out late, then?" said Garis.

"Guards are out looking for poachers by now," Juggler put in.

Dikon grinned. "Nothing to find now."

"Good." Garis sniffed. "You're sure there won't be any cooking smells left by morning?"

Dikon shook his head. "Don't ask impossibles. But we have a fairly good explanation about how I got hungry in the middle of the watch and so on." He frowned, and added, "We're going to have to be careful how often we run that one."

"Think it's time we put an end to scraping by and waiting for dark, do you?" said Garis.

"I didn't say that." Dikon's tone and words were cautious, but his face lightened at the question. He caught his breath and looked expectantly at Garis.

"Open the cells."

Soon the passage was jammed with prisoners, both men and women. Juggler wondered uneasily if this assembly could be heard outside the walls, but when he looked into a cell on the windowed side, he saw that the preparations for a meeting included a small troop under the direction of an angular, fair woman about Dikon's age, putting the bars in place and hanging layers of blankets over them.

The door they had come through had already acquired a similar muffling along the cracks, and so had the door at the far end of the passage. There were evidently prisoners locked in the level below who were thought loyal to Dale—or, at least, not likely to be loyal to Garis.

Meanwhile, Garis had worked his way down the passage, greeting people, asking questions about the hunting, their health, their news, their kinfolk, wishes, and worries. He came back again, with more of the same, then stood on tiptoe, for lack of a dais, and waved for silence. He took a deep breath, and told them of the plan for him to go in search of Bonefrost.

There was a murmur of approval. Bonefrost's limitations might worry Eldwin, but Garis's troop of prisoners liked the idea of magic on their side.

"When I get back—I'll send word," Garis finished. "Anyone outside then joins the outside party. Otherwise, you know the split. Enough of us outside to take the guards' attention as an assault, the rest inside to take them from behind when you hear sounds of the attack. And we win our freedom from Dale." He whirled around to direct his attention, and theirs, to Juggler. "Can you sing that?"

Juggler began to whistle, instead, a slow, sad tune. Garis gave him a sidelong look of confused dismay, but Juggler went on unheeding. Garis's looked changed to curiosity, and he remained silent.

The crowd hushed to be able to hear the quiet melody. Juggler went once through it, and then began to sing.

Oak ash elm yew
Once in spring the green leaves grew
Yew oak ash elm
Summer heat upon the realm
Elm yew oak ash
Red and gold in fire's flash
Ash elm yew oak
Killing cold and tyrant's yoke.

There was silence as Juggler finished. He let it hold a few heartbeats more, and then began to clap his hands. It sounded loud in the stillness. In a moment more, it *was* loud, as the others joined in, clapping with him. Juggler glanced again at the muffling around them. Having just made a giant human drum for himself to carry the rhythm of his song, he did not want interruptions from any extra, ill-timed audience. But the padding looked heavy enough to hold the sound.

He had a different tune, this time, higher and louder and demanding a chorus. After the first pause before the first "pigs" they had caught on, and were joining in with him to shout each verse-end.

> Sing of the mud that's down by the lake
> Where Dale of a day kept—pigs.
> Cares sent the noble down to the hollow
> To rest in a cool, refreshing wallow.
> I sadly fear that his son's a fake.
> You ought to go check with the—pigs.

> Norcote turncoat, raise the glass high,
> Drink to the prince of—pigs.
> None can deny it—I'll prove that he is.
> Look at his ears and the snout on his phiz.
> Look at the bristles, the tiny black eye.
> Look at the prince of—pigs.

> It follows the father of pigs is the king,
> Sire of the prince of — pigs.
> Like father like son—the wisdom of yore.
> The king of the pigs is a royal bore,
> Not worth discussing anymore.
> The king and the prince of—pigs.

The shout broke up in laughter and hooting. Juggler bowed and stepped back.

Before Garis could step forward again, Dikon shoved open the door, where he had been outside, keeping watch. Blankets popped free from the edges, flapped forward, and were grabbed up.

The prisoners vanished into their cells, stripping muffling with them as they went. The angular young woman met Dikon's eyes, and waited until he nodded. Spinning around, she scurried after the others, checking as she went for any signs of the assembly. Then she was gone, too.

Juggler, finding himself alone with Garis and Dikon, and presumably in danger, spun around to stare, first at Dikon and the door, and then at Garis. Neither of them seemed to be indicating which way he should run. Dikon's bulk and a blanket behind him, still filling the door-opening, concealed whatever might be about to come through it.

"No hurry," said Dikon. "I'm a very careful sentry."

"Oh," said Juggler, without much gratitude.

"Jailmaster won't be down for a few minutes," Dikon said. He plucked the remaining blanket down from the door-frame, and folded it neatly over one arm. "But his page went by—means it's time to go wake him, and time for mice to be in holes and out of the way."

"Thanks, Dikon," said Garis. He stretched, and the lack of a night's sleep seemed to have caught up with him. "I'd better go get some floors finished before breakfast, if I don't want to be out of a job." He embraced Dikon and started up the stairs.

Juggler hurried after him, with a wave to the tall young jailer. "Don't you have any plans for sleeping?"

"Yes, after breakfast. You'd better skip breakfast, though," Garis said.

"Why?" Juggler started to say, but then he realized that lack of sleep had caught up with him, too, and he was not as young as Garis.

"I'll save something for you."

Juggler glanced around to be sure they were by themselves, thought about it, and bowed.

"Don't do that," said Garis.

"I suppose you're right," said Juggler regretfully. He waved, and set off for his bed. The sun was rising outside. Inside, the darkness had changed to grey, rapidly giving way to gold as he reached the room. Juggler pulled off his clothes, relieved himself in the chamber pot, and stretched out on his pallet. He snuggled his face into the pillow and took up his interrupted sleep.

Chapter 3
Escape

When Bramble shook him awake near lunchtime, Juggler could not at first find any good reason for being conscious and getting up. At last it occurred to him that there was probably work he should be doing somewhere, although he could not, just at the moment, remember what it was or where it was. He sat up, blinked, and said, "Good morning?"

"Just barely. It's your turn to help the cooks." Bramble pointed at something repulsive on the floor by his pallet. "Was that supposed to be your breakfast?"

Juggler squinted his eyes against the daylight that seemed unreasonably bright in the air around him and discovered that the stuff was a plate with some biscuits and cheese on it. "I suppose." He reached down and picked up a biscuit. By the time he had swallowed it he had remembered himself. "You're right, I'm on duty. Thanks. I'll be down in a couple minutes."

The ewer was empty, so he could not wash his hands until he got down to the kitchen, but he took his comb from his pack and combed his beard and hair. Then he rummaged further into his pack and brought out a cake of glue, which he tucked into a pocket, and set off down the stairs to his work.

The head cook acknowledged his presence with a scowl. "Mind how you carve the roast," she said. She was firmly convinced that no one but herself and possibly her husband was worthy of shifting food she'd cooked from pan to platter to plate. She doubted that anyone but herself fully appreciated the beauty of her art, particularly when it came to the timing and serving of a roast.

Juggler dutifully minded his carving. Once the main crisis points had passed, he said, "Oh, by the way—"

The head cook had heard that tone of voice. She looked at her husband, who looked at Juggler and spotted the bulge in the pocket, which he then pointed out to his wife.

"Not in our fireplace!" they said, as one.

"Not till after we've cleaned up lunch," said Juggler, coaxingly. "And I'll burn some applewood and sweetgum to drive out the stink, if you give me some sweetgum. Besides, this handle's seen better days." He held up the carving knife and showed the split running up the grain.

They grudgingly agreed to let him have the use of the kitchen fire and a pan to melt the glue, and the gum for after, on condition that he fixed the knife.

After lunch had gone out to the court tables, food began going out to the servants, as well. As the sweets were paraded out to the court, the meats were spread in the servants' hall. Juggler and the cooks stayed in the kitchen, around a small and steamy table by the fire for theirs. Clearing up was already beginning around them as they ate. Juggler filled his plate again, and put an extra plate over it to make it clear that he had plans for this food, so that no one would clear it away for him (with comments on shocking waste, if it happened to be the Steward) while he was at work with the scullery crew.

Once the cleaning up was completed, and the cooks had retired for a nap, to be followed by contemplation of the arrangements for supper, Juggler set his glue on to melt, and used the time to take the extra food he had set aside, and go with it up to the servants' quarters to get his tool-kit and leave lunch for Garis. As he had expected, he found Garis fast asleep, with a left-over clean rush fallen on the floor beside him.

Juggler spent the next hour making his assorted repairs. In addition to gluing things that needed to be glued, he pounded two bent spoons straight. A third he set aside as beyond what his skill and tools would let him do. It would have to go to a smith. Finally, he tightened the strings he had wrapped around all the glued items so that they would stay put while the glue hardened, took some new pegs he had whittled to the spinsters' workroom to fasten in the loom, glued and tied them in place, and returned to the kitchen to clear away the evidence of his work. The rotten smell of fish-glue lingered, but he had put sweet-burning wood and gum on the fire as he had promised, and those would do to hide the smell of the glue until it finished spreading out and was gone.

Then he swallowed, wishing he had something more needing to be done instantly, to put off the other errand. But he didn't, so he went in search of the king. He found him in his study, in council with an ambassador from a country beyond the eastern waste. They were deep in conversation, arguing over trade rights. It occurred to Juggler to wonder how trade in that direction— to the east, farther off than Melibos—might affect the unease between Emmering and Melibos, but the ambassador either was not asking questions on the subject, or was asking in terms Juggler did not understand.

He did not care, either. The king was busy, and that was good enough for the moment. He accepted the excuse for a delay, backed off from the study door, and went and whittled out two pawns for a chess set.

When he tried again, though, the ambassador had finished his business, and the way was clear for Juggler to go in. The door was ajar, and he could see the king leaning back on his cushions, one hand thrown over his eyes. The sun's movement had brought him into the light. The hand protecting his eyes from the glare looked as if it were on fire with the blaze of gold and emerald in his rings. But as Juggler touched the door he heard Dianor, repeating an old story of a witch's granddaughter and her sweetheart. Juggler started to retreat again.

Dale caught the movement, and beckoned him in.

"So they built a house of foam and fish-scales in the middle of the river," Dianor said, "and if they are not gone they are living there still."

Dale nodded his thanks, and drew back into the shade.

Juggler looked at him curiously, but there was no way to tell from the king's expression if listening to a simple story was his own idea of amusement, or something he had accepted because he thought it might amuse Dianor.

"Well, Juggler," Dale said, "what about the lute?"

"It needs special strings, your majesty. No one makes them here. The nearest supply is over in Melibos. May I have your leave to go there?"

Dianor was looking at him with the puzzled frown of half recognition, at his voice.

"You're welcome to my leave, but it won't carry much weight in Melibos," Dale said.

"I won't show it there. But I imagine I'll need it on the way back."

The king nodded. "Dianor, will you find me some ink and parchment?"

She went to the cupboard he had pointed out and pulled it open. It was evidently old, for the panels were carved with heads of wheat, and she had to tug to get it open.

Juggler added as casually as he could, "I'm not much of a fighter, if trouble comes along."

The king raised one eyebrow, looking skeptical.

"And I won't have the lute with me," said Juggler, by way of answer to the look. "Could I take one of the younger servants on the way?"

"I suppose so. Which one?"

"I think his name's Garis."

A shade passed over the king's face at the name.

Juggler managed to look blankly patient.

"Very well," the king said at last. Dianor set a writing desk before him, and he smiled at her. He took the pen and wrote, "Juggler and Garis, servants of the king, have the king's leave to travel in Emmering or beyond it." He signed it, and scattered sand over the wet ink. Then he lit a stick of sealing wax at the fire, and swore as the flame went out as soon as he took it away.

Dianor laughed. "Uncle, let me." She turned the heavy wax slowly, so that it melted evenly around the wick, and cupped the flame with her free hand as she turned back to the parchment. Soon there was a thin circle of liquid wax gleaming on the page. The king set his seal-ring over it. When he raised his hand a sheaf of wheat over curling waves stood out in the red wax. He hesitated as he shook the sand off, but after a moment's more thought he gave the page to Juggler.

Juggler took it and rolled it into a cylinder narrow enough to hold comfortably in his hand, taking care not to roll it so tightly that the wax and seal cracked. He bowed, and left the room, struggling against the urge to run or, by way of alternative, show the elaborate courtesy of walking out backwards, so that he could watch the king's face as he went.

Dale rubbed at his beard as Juggler left. The closing of the door seemed to jar something in him. He snapped his fingers and pointed his hand at the empty doorway. "Garis! Yes, I've seen the boy around. His name is bad enough, but his face—"

"What's the matter?" said Dianor, putting away the writing desk.

"Why, it's the same name—" He stopped, and let Dianor fill in the history for herself. The king shook his head, continuing the thought. "And to make it worse, he has the look of the family in his face."

"Are you sure?" said Dianor. "They're all dead, aren't they?"

"They are," said the king. "But what a thunderbolt the boy could be if one of the nobles wanted to make a figurehead of him!" Dale frowned, tapping his fingers against his knee. "No, he mustn't be allowed to wander where he likes."

"What are you going to do?" Dianor's voice was calm, but she was staring at the king.

"Nothing so terrible as that," he said, meeting her look. "Let me see. You have some lands to the north. I'll send him to your estate and let him work there. Your steward's faithful to me, and I'll tell him to see to it that your unlucky-featured servant is kept within doors."

"But that's not fair."

"I can't afford to be fair, Dianor," said the king quietly. "I can't have him walking about for any to see and think of using. In fact—" But the king stopped without finishing his sentence, and went to call a guard.

Dianor hesitated a moment, while the king's footsteps went away. Then she fled from the room and ran all the way to the servants' quarters, arriving too breathless to speak.

Garis, looking groggy from his daylight sleep, was awake and sitting on his pallet, eating cheese, and trying to pay attention to Juggler.

"It's all right," Juggler was saying, "we can go." He flourished the rolled paper and let it drop open to show off the circle of red wax. Then he saw Dianor out of the corner of his eye, jumped round to face her, and bowed politely. "Yes, my lady?" he said, rolling the pass back up again.

Garis managed a bow while still sitting.

Dianor said, panting, "I remembered. Voice. So I owe you a favor."

Now it was Garis's turn to be puzzled, not quite recognizing Dianor from her voice. He could not see what favor Dale's niece could owe Juggler.

"My uncle," said Dianor, and stopped there, although she had her breath back and could have gone on. She was betraying him.

Juggler had already guessed what she had to say. He had not liked the expression on the king's face when Garis's name had come up, and so he had hurried as much as dared, for fear someone would show up to stop them. "Doesn't like Garis's looks?" he said, to spare Dianor further explanation.

Dianor nodded in agreement.

Garis shoved himself off the bed and stood up. "See if you can get two horses out beyond the wall," he said to Juggler. "I'll meet you outside."

"How?" said Dianor, practically.

"I'll manage somehow, my lady," he said. He did not sound very sure of it. He could hardly go up the poachers' ladder by day, and hiding until dark would be a problem.

"You're you!" said Dianor suddenly.

"Who?" said Garis. But in the same moment he recognized her voice and understood. "Yes," he replied.

For a moment they stared at each other, recognizing the shadowed face in the daylight one, and wanting to be back in shadow and unaware of new dangers.

Then Dianor took a breath and pursed her lips, thinking. "The stable backs the wall. I'll go get my mare and stop by the side to check the girth. Meet me there, and you should be able to get on the roof by standing on Emerald, and from there to the wall. Then you bring two horses out, Juggler, and we'll meet on the outside, and Garis can step down on one."

"You're forgetting the ditch," said Garis. "It'd be a drop, not a step."

"Best you can do, and you're wasting time," said Dianor.

"Yes."

Garis and Dianor hurried out, taking separate ways.

Juggler waited a minute, to give Dianor time with her Emerald. It was a foolhardy scheme, but she was probably right. It was the best they could do, by day. If a guard saw them she could claim the odd gymnastics were a game to amuse her, so that getting caught in the act would not make matters any worse. And getting caught at all by the king's order could be lethal for Garis. If they could have been sure that Garis would be put in the dungeon, they could have waited capture, but even that might give away too much, when he escaped.

Juggler tried to stop thinking about it, and set off for the stable.

Outside, it was chilly again. The sun was still well up in the sky, but a ghostly-looking slice of white moon was visible in the west.

At the stable, a single ostler was more or less on duty. He had found himself a spot in the sun and out of the wind, and was sitting on a bench with his hands in his lap and his legs stretched out.

"Afternoon," said Juggler. "Can I take two horses out?" He held up the king's note of permission.

"Horses," said the ostler mournfully. "Never a moment's rest for man nor beast. His highness and a whole troop away this morning on patrol, and her highness off for fresh air, if you please, just now, and you want two? Fresh air," he repeated to himself, and shook his head.

"I can saddle them myself, if you'd rather," said Juggler.

The ostler gave him a sharp look. "Know how?" he asked suspiciously. He didn't enjoy obliging people, but he objected still more to having horses ill-treated.

"Yes."

"Good," said the ostler, and went back to contemplation of nothing in particular.

The strongest and fastest horses had gone with Lyndred's patrol, of course. Juggler was light enough to ride a mare, and found a gelding to take for Garis. As he started getting the second saddle on, he heard a guard outside speaking to the ostler.

"Know a lad called Garis?"

"Garis?" The ostler considered it. "Aye."

"He here?"

"No."

"If he comes round, send him back. King wants to see him."
The guard poked his head inside the stable, wrinkling his nose
at the smell. "Juggler, is it?" He opened his eyes wide, peering
into the darkness, and after a moment made out both Juggler
and the pair of horses he was leading by the reins. "You'll be
putting one of those back."

"Wait a minute," Juggler protested. "What am I supposed to
do? I'm going to need a companion on the road."

"I don't know about that," said the guard.

"It's safer travelling with someone than alone," Juggler
pointed out.

The guard shrugged. "You could take the spare and maybe
find someone in the village, if that's any help."

"It'll do," said Juggler, willing the guard not to think of
climbing up on the roof for a complete inspection. He pulled
the girths tight, swung himself up, and set off on the mare,
leading the gelding.

The ostler was still contemplating nothing.

The guard frowned and stepped to the other side of the door,
evidently checking to be sure that Garis was not clinging to
the gelding's other side. It wasn't likely—the horse would have
been nervous with such an unaccustomed rider—but he was
conscientious, and went on watching carefully until Juggler was
out of the stable. He was kicking at suspicious heaps of straw
as Juggler rode out of sight.

Over the grounds, out the gate, back following the curve of
the wall. It seemed a long way.

Finally Juggler came in sight of Dianor, standing at her
mare's head, but wearing a riding skirt she must have picked
up in the stable. She looked from the little distance like a broken
porcelain figure unsuitably re-bodied, with the fine linen of a
yellow dress rising out of the shapeless blob of the wide leather
skirt.

Then Garis appeared, sliding over the top of the wall and
down the side until he was hanging at full-length. It was slippery
with moss there. He had all he could do to keep hold, and he
could not look down.

"Not yet," said Dianor, backing the horse a pace to put the
saddle directly below Garis's feet. "Ready," she said.

Garis let go. For half a moment he stood balanced on horseback. Then Emerald reared, tearing the reins loose from Dianor's hands. Garis tried to throw his arms around the neck looming up against him as his feet skidded on air, but he missed, and fell to the ground. He landed on his feet, dropped to his knees, tried to jump up to grab for the reins, and sprawled forward.

"Emerald!" said Dianor.

The mare stopped, looked around cautiously, and came nosing her way back with an innocent air to see what had happened, as if it had been nothing to do with her.

Juggler finished covering the space between them and swung off as hastily as he could manage, while still keeping hold of two sets of reins. The two mares and the gelding looked at each other, and seemed to take comfort in company. They stamped once each, but seemed willing to believe that the humans were behaving acceptably, though oddly.

Garis got to his knees.

Juggler put both sets of reins over one arm and went to Garis. He started to ask "Are you all right," but Garis shook his head impatiently. There was no time to look.

Garis held up his hands. Juggler and Dianor took them and pulled him up. Then Dianor took the reins while Juggler helped Garis to mount. He set off at a trot, turned pale, pulled back to a walk, and headed the horse across the grounds to the high road.

Dianor looked ruefully at her hands, cut where Emerald had pulled loose, but reached under the riding skirt to hitch the skirt of her dress back up again, and mounted Emerald. Juggler scrambled back into saddle as well, and it took them only a few moments to catch up to Garis.

From the other side of the high road, several of the villagers looked up as Lady Dianor and her escort rode by. But it seemed to be idle curiosity. There were some grins at what seemed to be Garis's clumsy riding, and nothing more. No search squad had come out of the palace yet.

Dianor nudged Emerald alongside the gelding. "Are you all right?" Dianor asked Garis.

"No, but I don't think I broke anything. The right foot's sprained, maybe. As soon as we get round that curve in the road, so we're out of sight, I'd like to stop a bit."

Dianor nodded, and they went on in silence.

When they stopped, Juggler dismounted. "Let's get the shoe off," he said.

Garis nodded, and clenched his teeth while Juggler undid the latchets and eased the shoe off as gently as he could.

"Can you move your toes?" Juggler asked.

Garis demonstrated.

Juggler touched the ankle. Nothing happened. He touched the instep.

"Ai!" Garis's breath caught in his throat.

"I think you're right," said Juggler. "It's sprained. What can we tie it up with?"

"Hem of my dress," said Dianor. "No one'll see it under the riding skirt, anyhow." She turned up the edge of the skirt, took her eating-knife from her belt, and was about to slice off a bandage.

"Expensive," said Garis. The border of the dress was embroidered with acorns of red and silver.

Dianor's eyes gleamed as if she would have enjoyed the destruction, but then she nodded and held out the knife to Juggler, turning up the embroidery against the riding skirt. Looking somewhat embarrassed, he helped her hold back both layers of fabric, and cut enough off the plain yellow of the underdress to make a good-sized bandage.

Juggler proceeded to tie up Garis's sprain with most of it, and saved out enough to go around the little cuts on Dianor's hands. He did not try to fit the shoe back on the swollen foot, but handed it up to Garis, who tied it to his belt.

"How does that feel?"

"Better. Should be all right for riding." He looked shyly at Dianor. "Hadn't you better go back and have your hands seen to properly?"

"No, it's nothing." She laughed. "And I wouldn't want to explain how it happened."

They set off at a canter, as that was a smoother gait, and trotting was too painful for Garis. When the horses tired they slowed to a walk and then alternated the paces. They made reasonable speed that way, without winding the horses.

If the king wanted to press the search hard enough, he would find out which way they had gone as soon as the search got around to asking in the village. Catching up to them would be no great matter. But it would take time, and soon it would be dark. Behind them the pale moonslice turned to silver. It would give light enough to follow a road, but not enough to find anyone easily if a fugitive heard people behind and went off the road to hide. They were safe for the time being.

As they slowed again to a walk, Garis said reluctantly, "Perhaps you should be turning back, my lady."

"Perhaps I should," Dianor said placidly, "but I told the ostler I was going to ride out and meet the people roundabout and perhaps visit somewhere overnight—and that's what I'm going to do."

"Rosewind will worry," said Juggler.

"People have to let me be a grown-up sometime." She did not say who beside her nurse might be included among the people, and they did not ask.

They met few travelers along the way. The hostility growing between Dale and Wyrond had stopped official traffic from Melibos, and slowed the trade along the river. The weather had been dry enough for the road to be dusty. The absence of traffic allowed them to ride abreast of each other. If they'd had to ride one after the other, the ones behind would have been choking on the dust. As it was, they had fresh air for all, and could talk without straining. Animals were shy of the road, and few wildflowers had yet come into bloom, but the progress of trees coming into leaf and birds returning to the northlands gave them enough to talk about without getting into touchier matters—such as the king.

As the day wore on, Garis spoke less. He had more to hide, and the pain in his foot gradually took more of his attention.

Toward sunset, they came in sight of an inn. Dianor pulled up and looked at her companions. "What do you think?"

"I think we could," said Juggler slowly. "If there's a pursuit, they can't help making a noise searching, and we could get out."

"I think we have to," said Garis. Speaking was by now some effort for him.

As they drew near, they could see people inside drinking or eating or talking, but evidently no more travelers were expected for the day. The door was closed, although not barred, and there was no one in sight to take the horses.

Juggler dismounted and held Garis's horse steady while he eased his sprained foot up over the saddle, then hopped to the ground. The horse gave a nicker of protest at this unorthodox procedure, but was trained well enough to hold still for it, in spite of disapproving. Juggler started to help Garis inside, then stopped, trying to figure out what to do with the horses.

"Go ahead," said Dianor. "I'll take them round back to the stable."

They tried to bow, by way of thanks, but it was awkward to manage, and Dianor took away the need for it by gathering up the reins and vanishing around the corner of the inn.

Leaning on Juggler's shoulder, Garis hopped to the inn-door. Juggler edged it open. Inside were tables and benches, several occupied by men wearing the badge of the army, and a few by people who seemed to be local farmers. Their arrival did not seem to rouse more than reasonable interest.

A bench ran along most of the four walls, except on one side, where there was a fireplace, and the part of the back occupied by cupboards and a door to the stairwell and the kitchen. The bench was empty where they had come in, no doubt because it was the draftiest spot, but under the circumstances it was convenient. Juggler deposited Garis on the bench and looked around for someone to be asking their pleasure.

After a moment he spotted him. The innkeeper was sitting at a small table by the cupboards, going over his accounts on a tally-board. He was a burly man with grey hair which might once have been red, and his hands looked too big to handle the tally counters as expertly as they did. Juggler hesitated, not wanting to draw further attention by calling out, but the innkeeper looked up then, and set down the board. He shoved himself off his stool and came to them with a professional smile. "Evening, sirs. What's your pleasure?"

Juggler was hungry enough to want something more food-like than beer to drink. "Buttermilk, three suppers, two rooms, and a longish strip of clean cloth."

"And a glass of spirits," said Garis, hoping strong drink would dull the pain in his foot.

The innkeeper looked them over, taking in their cheap clothing and the shoe Garis was not wearing. "Yes, sirs. And may I see an earnest fee?"

"No," said Garis. "Madame our lady—" He stopped and pointed at his foot by way of explaining why he was not the one doing the chore. "—will be in as soon as the horses are stabled, and she'll see to it. There's someone there to help her?"

"Servant-lad," he answered. "You'll forgive me, sirs, if I wait till she's here." He fixed his eyes on them steadily, ready to ignore any protest.

"Trade's bad, is it?" said Garis, sympathetically, looking up to meet his gaze.

The innkeeper shrugged and unbent a little, seeing that they understood his need for caution. "I'm keeping open. It could be better. Begging your pardon, I'm supposed to ask where folk are going."

Juggler brought out their pass. The innkeeper glanced at it, and gave it back. "Mentions no lady."

"No," said Juggler. "She had a mind to see the River and take advantage of the escort. Not for us to refuse."

The innkeeper shrugged again. "Well, I asked." He did not seem to consider these enquiries good for trade. "I'll go get things ready for you. Begging your pardon, I can't serve them till I see coin." He considered Garis. "I'll advance you the bandage, though."

"Pity we had to show the pass," said Juggler, as the innkeeper left them and went out to the kitchen. "He'll remember us."

Garis leaned his head against the wall. "He would anyway. Comes with the job."

After a moment the innkeeper returned with some long, clean rags. He pointed to a small table which was empty, to show that they could take it. It was empty because it was on the side of the room away from the fireplace. It was cold, but quieter than the warmer spots, and warmer than sitting on the part of the bench by the door.

The innkeeper meandered across the room, ready to be stopped by guests who wanted to order more. Several took advantage of the opportunity, but at length he disappeared again into the kitchen.

Juggler helped Garis to a seat by their table, then took the makeshift bandage off and bound the foot up again more firmly from the new supply. He looked about for some place to discard the crumpled yellow linen.

"Waste not," said Garis, and took the strip of yellow away from him and belted it around his middle. The color was bright against his drab clothes. He pulled his tunic up a little so that it bloused over the linen and hid most of it.

All the soldiers looked up suddenly.

Someone was coming down the stairs. He turned into the main room and made a snorting noise of surprise.

Garis and Juggler looked up.

Prince Lyndred was staring at them.

Chapter 4:
Into Melibos

Lyndred called through the other door into the kitchen, "Any chance of supper?" and added to one of the soldiers, "How long was I asleep?"

"Yes, your highness," and "Not long, your highness," came the answers.

The innkeeper came out at once, carrying what was obviously one of the suppers Juggler bespoke. He looked sternly at Juggler and Garis in case they had any intention of objecting. Then he gaped in bewilderment as Lyndred sat down with them at the little table.

"What brings you out this far?" Lyndred said to Juggler. "You're into patrol country. Oh, thanks," he added, as the innkeeper put the tray in front of him, "and I'd like some smallbeer, too." It was a simple enough meal, but it made the others' mouths water as Lyndred took a spoonful of frumity porridge sweetened with blackberry jam and then a bite of a slice of blue cheese. He gave a sigh. "That's good. It was a long day," he told Juggler. "Threat of invasion down by the merchant-town, or at rate a substantial raid. Wasn't, though. It was nothing." He scowled.

The innkeeper, back again with a mug and a pitcher of smallbeer, and about to set them down in front of Lyndred, stopped short and waited cautiously for direction.

The prince held out his hand.

The innkeeper put the mug into it and slid the pitcher into place in front of him, almost as smoothly as if there had been no break in the rhythm of setting them out.

Juggler raised his eyebrows as Lyndred stretched out his arm to pour himself a mugful of smallbeer.

There was dried blood on the prince's sleeve.

Lyndred glanced down at the sleeve, shrugged, and took two gulps of his drink. "Almost nothing. Couple of smugglers." He took another mouthful of porridge, then turned to the business at hand. He looked from one to the other of them, and settled his attention on Juggler. "Well?"

The innkeeper had moved away to what was ostensibly out of earshot, but the suspicious expression came back to his face at Lyndred's question. The change caught Juggler's eye, and he stuttered instead of answering.

Lyndred turned to see where he was looking, and laughed. "Oh, I expect I can vouch for him," he told the innkeeper. "A musician." He started to turn his attention to Garis, but then looked back at Juggler. "No lessons in the field, thank you," he said.

Juggler laughed politely.

The innkeeper bowed to the prince and disappeared into the kitchen.

Lyndred turned back to them. "So I vouch for you. But you still have to account for yourselves."

"Lute-strings, your highness."

"Oh," said Lyndred expressionlessly.

"And a companion on the road for safety's sake."

Lyndred nodded, accepting the explanation of Juggler's companion, but still looked doubtful.

"And no lessons at all while I'm gone," Juggler pointed out.

The prince laughed, and took another bite of cheese. He chewed it slowly, considering. "I forbid it," he said at last. "What you need for safety's sake is a full escort, Juggler, and I can't spare it."

"Lyndred, what are you doing here?" It was Dianor, at last. She had not trusted horses in her care to the stableboy. Her riding skirt and the top of her dress were covered with horsehairs. She brushed absently at one sleeve, not much minding, and looked quizzically at the prince.

He jumped up, moved his stool for her to take, and nodded to the nearest of his soldiers to bring an empty stool to their table for him.

The innkeeper was back with the other two suppers. Without a blink he put one of them in front of Dianor and the other in front of Garis. "Ready in a moment," he said to Juggler, by way of consolation, serving him nothing more than the mug of buttermilk he'd asked for.

Dianor and Garis both started to set their cheeses in front of him, and then started to exchange the extra cheese for porridge together, as well.

Juggler resolved the surplus of generosity by grabbing Dianor's cheese and Garis's porridge, with a heartfelt but hasty "Thanks" before the first mouthful, and a nod of the head as a substitute for a bow to Dianor as he started chewing.

Lyndred waited impatiently as they went through these courtesies. "What brings you here, my lady?" he said, as soon as she was free to answer.

"Emerald," she said. "But I asked you first."

"Patrol," he said briefly, looking annoyed at her quibbles. "What *purpose* brought you?" His blue eyes met her dark ones. He could not demand answers of his cousin as he could of his servants, but he could go on asking.

She was silent a moment. "I don't think you understand this," she said, "but I've been in prison all my life."

"If that's a riddle, you're right," he said. "I don't understand it."

"I mean...I've hardly been anywhere, and everywhere I've been there was someone to watch what I do and tell me not to do it. Nurse, my teachers, the king. Even you, Cousin. I'm always being warned to behave, to stay within doors—on my estate, in the school, in the palace. I wanted to see the Longwater, and they were going—" She nodded at Juggler and Garis. "—and so I went with."

"They're not going," said Lyndred. "I don't think it's safe." He poured himself another mug of smallbeer and finished off the cheese.

Dianor's back stiffened.

"Consider, your highness," said Juggler, "if I die defending my lady at the river, you're free of music lessons."

Lyndred grinned reluctantly and swallowed his mouthful of cheese. "That's tempting, but it might give me the same results if you don't have the strings to mend that noise-box of yours. Let's have your charter." He held out his hand.

Juggler thought of denying that he had one, but the innkeeper could have given him the lie immediately, and even if he didn't, Lyndred would find out later and could send word round to his patrols revoking it. He handed it over. Lyndred read it through carefully, noting the authenticity of signature and seal, and tried to tear it. Parchment being strong, it resisted. Annoyed, he took out his knife and slit it enough for him to tear it into four pieces. He handed the pieces over to a soldier, who put them in the fire.

Dianor was pale with anger.

The others in the inn could not help but notice. They were not eating, drinking, or talking. They were not watching the prince and his cousin quarrel, either. What they did not see they heard all the more keenly.

It was bad for business.

The innkeeper swooped in with the remaining food, and distributed it accurately between Juggler and his two benefactors.

Lyndred scowled at the silence around them. "Here," he said to the innkeeper, and handed him six half-golds. "Drinks round the house—and my thanks for a good day's work to my men and good luck to the rest." He looked over the soldiers and added quietly, "But if Otterwort asks for spirits or ale, water it. He's had enough and too much."

The innkeeper tossed one of the coins in the air, testing its weight.

Lyndred gave him a look of astonishment.

The innkeeper turned red and pocketed the prince's coins without further examination.

The announcement of free drinks brought conversation and a reasonable flow of orders back to the room. The conversation sounded a little forced to begin with. A good number of the listeners obviously realized that they were being told to direct their ears elsewhere. But as the drinks began to arrive, and more food with them, the conversation grew louder and more natural.

Lyndred looked tired, in spite of his nap. He drank some of his smallbeer, looked at what was left of his food, and put one elbow on the table so that he could rest his chin on his hand. He pointed at Juggler and Garis. "Tomorrow escort Lady Dianor home. The music can wait, and the boats at Merchanton will be in better order in a few days, anyway. If you reach the palace at noon...." He stopped to calculate. "No, I won't send a report with you. I sent a messenger today already, and I should be back myself by sunset."

"Yes, your highness," said Juggler, winning a look of reproach from Dianor.

"I'm sorry, Cousin," said Lyndred, and added to Juggler, "I hold you responsible, and you will suffer for it if she does not appear."

"Yes, your highness," Juggler said again.

Dianor looked ready to begin quarreling in earnest.

Juggler shifted uneasily on his stool, not looking directly either at the cousins or at Garis.

If Lyndred was angry or worried enough about her he might spare one of his soldiers to shepherd them back.

Garis said abruptly, "What about a song for the company, Juggler?"

Juggler pushed his seat back and glanced at Lyndred for permission.

The prince, without much enthusiasm, waved him to go ahead.

Juggler made him a bow in token of what was, under the circumstances, generous forbearance. Lyndred was not in a mood to enjoy a concert.

The prince accepted his bow, saying, "Sooner you than me," and withdrew his attention from them, falling into a reverie, except that he glanced over at Dianor now and again.

Juggler made another bow, to the company as a whole, and sauntered to the middle of the room. He turned once around, centering attention on himself, and began to sing.

The stars are bright. The sky's alight.
I'm lost on a shining road.
But I can wait to find my gait.
The turn of time is slowed.
The sun goes down, and the wind goes down,
And the river goes down to the sea.
The moon is up, and so's my cup.
Come have a drink with me.

If I haven't found a ride to the ground
Walking the welkin's way
I'll maybe stop on a mountain-top
To look for yesterday.

The sun goes down, and the wind goes down,
And the river goes down to the sea.
The moon is up, and so's my cup.
Come have a drink with me.

If I don't return, no hearts should burn.
A rainbow burns in the blue.
Never think I've nothing to drink—
I drink your health to you.
The sun goes down, and the wind goes down,
And the river goes down to the sea.
The moon is up, and so's my cup.
Come have a drink with me.

Juggler bowed, to a scattering of applause. One of the locals said, "Another, friend?"

"Fair's fair. I took my turn. What about yourself?"

"Don't mind." The other swallowed the last of her beer, cleared her throat, and launched into, "I haven't a word to say against soup." This was a song that most of them knew, so most of the rest joined in, and other familiar songs followed.

Juggler beckoned to the innkeeper. "Will you show us where we're to sleep? My ears would like to stay and listen, but my eyes are against it." He glanced at Dianor and Garis.

Dianor listened a few minutes longer, half tempted to sit up a while longer downstairs, then smiled at Garis and stood, clearing the way for him to be moved, and edged the stool out of her way so that she could go with them.

Juggler and the innkeeper went to the table and helped Garis up.

Lyndred looked ruefully at Dianor as she went after them, but did not try to speak to her.

At the turning of the stairs they paused for breath. Garis looked back down at the soldiers crowding the benches. "We wouldn't have to have two whole rooms to ourselves. If you're displacing someone for us—"

The innkeeper shook his head. "King doesn't spend money on rooms for soldiers. Pays a little for floor-space in the hall for them to sleep, and they get some food and drink. But what with trade with Melibos down so much, we don't get traders coming through as they used to. We take what we can get."

"Traders spend more?" Garis suggested.

The innkeeper gave a snort of emphatic agreement, then waggled one hand by way of qualification. "Depending on how the trading's going. And with the king's men I get a little something."

They trudged up the rest of the stairs. On the floor above, he led them to two rooms next to one another. They were small and plain, holding each a bed, a pot, and a stand with tallow candles, basin, and ewer. There was no sign of bugs or rot underneath the mattresses. The innkeeper, with a look of weary patience, held Garis while they checked.

Juggler took Garis back and helped him to sit down on their bed.

The innkeeper held the door open to escort Dianor the half-dozen steps to her own room. She waved him away. He shrugged and left them.

Dianor leaned against the door-jamb. "So you're going to take me to the palace tomorrow?"

Juggler hesitated.

"We could hardly say anything else," Garis remarked. "But we don't have to do it."

Dianor looked surprised and then thoughtful. Garis was not promising not to take her back. But he didn't sound as if he had any intention of trying. She took a deep breath, thought some more, and let it out. "Thank you, friends. Good night."

She left them, and they got ready for bed without further conversation. The sheets were cold, and they lay shivering, waiting for the warmth of their bodies to accumulate.

The inn was well built, with solid walls. They could not hear the noise from the common room below. Wind in the oaks and maples could be heard through the little window, and some owls were calling. Once a wolf cried out. Then they were asleep.

Juggler's dreams were uneasy. He was cold, and kept dreaming of a cold sword. The blade shone white in his dreams, but when morning came he could not remember what else had been in the dreams. He woke at the first light, in the false dawn before the sun appeared. The sky was grey and cloudless.

Juggler turned over, intending to go back to sleep, but in the process of stretching and trying to keep himself in the cover of the blankets, he wound up kicking Garis, who gave out a yelp. By then they were both fully awake.

"Sorry," said Juggler.

"Oh, well," said Garis. He looked around the room. "I don't suppose the provisions for guests include a razor?"

Juggler rubbed the sand from his eyes and looked about the room. There was no more to see than there had been the night before. He grunted at the chill as he slid out from under the covers. He hugged himself for a moment against the morning, then went to the stand, poured some water, and began to wash his face. "Let it grow."

Garis rubbed his chin and sniffed resentfully at him. "I'll look like a dog with the mange."

"You'll survive. How's the foot?"

"Better. Swelling's gone down. I can put my shoe on." Garis set his feet on the floor and leaned forward cautiously to put a little weight on them. He leaned back. "Won't do. But I think I could walk with a stick."

"I'll see if I can get one." Juggler made his way downstairs, trailing a hand against the wall to guide himself. The torches were out, and little of the grey light had found its way into the hall.

At the foot of the staircase he peeped into the common room. Lyndred's troop was asleep on the floor. Rather than cross among them, hoping for good luck in not treading on anyone, he hunted about, turning beneath the stairs, and found a little passageway that led him to the kitchen.

There, a woman was dividing dough into loaves. The warm smell of the dough filled the room. She was broader than the innkeeper, and almost as tall, as Juggler could see when she straightened up to inspect him. The look on her face—watchful and overworked and conscious of her authority—marked her as the innkeeper's wife. "Morning," she said, sparing him a glance.

"Good morning," he answered. "Could we get a cane, Mistress, or a walking staff? And if we could take some food with us—"

She shook her head, and began putting the loaves into pans. "Your lady took care of all that. Thought you'd want a proper crutch, though." She nodded at a corner. A stick with an armrest across the top was leaning against the wall.

"Oh! Thank you."

"Stableboy, he got his leg broken once. Last year, that was." She reflected. "Year before, maybe." She looked disapprovingly at Juggler. "Best hurry along. She's waiting outside."

"Thank you, Mistress." Juggler hurried obediently to take his prize upstairs to Garis and found him standing, his weight on one leg, and leaning against the wall for balance, just settling his tunic into place. "You ready? Lady Dianor seems to've gone round for the horses already."

"Blast!" said Garis.

Juggler gave him a surprised look.

Garis shrugged. "I was hoping to sneak out before she woke up. It'd let her get an escort that's actually going to be able to go with her back to the castle."

"She doesn't want to go back," Juggler pointed out.

Garis waved a hand impatiently, not accepting the objection.

"Well, why not?—as far as the river, anyway," Juggler asked.

Garis said in a low voice, "Later on, she won't be glad of any help she gave me."

"Oh." Garis was, after all, trying to overthrow her uncle. Dianor wasn't helping them escape because she wanted Garis on the throne. It was just that she thought Dale was wrong in planning to shut Garis up as a danger to the throne—which Garis was.

Garis looked at the crutch for a moment, and then held out his hand for it. He stood up, tested his weight on it, and started awkwardly down the stairs.

The innkeeper's wife was putting the loaves on to bake. She identified them by sound, sparing only a glance away from the oven to be sure of the identification, and gave them a shrug of a shoulder by way of a farewell and good speed.

Outside, it was almost sunrise. Dianor was sitting on the stoop, with her riding skirt folded under her for a cushion, watching colors in the east turn from pinks to oranges. Their horses were tied to the post next to the stoop.

"Good morning," she said. "Is it all right?" This question evidently meant the crutch, and not her presence ready to go on with them, but a hint of mischief in her eyes suggested that she knew well enough that she would have been left behind if she had not managed to be first out the door.

"Yes, thank you, my lady," said Garis, with some embarrassment. He could not quite manage to be sorry that she was still beside them, and for a moment his face lit up as his eyes met hers.

She answered with a chuckle, and he looked away, still more embarrassed.

Juggler untied the horses, and they mounted. Garis held the crutch across his saddle, looking with alarm to both sides to see if he was in danger of hitting his companions, which he was.

Juggler's mare shied away. Dianor coaxed Emerald into a quieter step to the side, out of danger. "Like a spear," she suggested.

Garis tucked the end of the crutch into the hole in the stirrup meant for a hunting spear, and rested the top against his shoulder. With a spear, it would have looked gallant. With a crutch, the effect was not quite the same. He rubbed his chin. "Your escort, my lady," he said glumly.

She grinned and swung Emerald around towards the road.

Garis rode beside her, and Juggler, a little slower to get his mare started and turned, followed behind them. The morning dew would hold the dust of the road down for a little while yet. As they entered the road Dianor turned east, but Garis turned west, away from the light.

"Hey!" said Dianor.

He looked over his shoulder at her, his eyes squinted against the brightness. Juggler hesitated and reined the mare in, not taking either direction.

"I'm going to see the Longwater. Escort me," said Dianor told them firmly.

"Yes, I was afraid of that," said Garis. "But even if you won't let us escort you partway back and—"

"No," she interrupted.

"No," Garis agreed, accepting her intention. "But we still want to be seen starting back, if there are travelers on the road who might be stopping here. I think the prince would think to question them."

"What's the good of that?" she argued. "We'd just be seen going the other way once we headed east."

Garis was taken aback. He had not thought far enough ahead, and he hesitated, trying to find a way to adjust his thoughts to the complication of Lyndred's intentions—and Dianor's. He looked to Juggler for suggestions, if he had any, but Juggler shook his head.

"I know!" Dianor exclaimed after a moment. She turned Emerald west, and set off on the castle road.

Her "escort" followed, looking confused.

Dianor looked back at them. "The Gillybranch," she said.

They looked doubtful, but came along.

By the time the sun was visible through treetops, they had reached the bridge where the road crossed the Gillybranch. It was a creek, sometimes called a river as a matter of courtesy. In summers it went dry, and a tall man could cross it on foot, even where it was deepest, most of the year. In spring, however, it was full and running fast.

Garis reined in at the middle of the bridge, and stopped, looking up and down the Branch on both sides. Even though it was full, near the edges it would still be shallow for long stretches.

"There," said Dianor suddenly, pointing across the water and a few yards upstream from where they were. She had spotted the clear patch which had been one side of the ford before the bridge was raised.

Across the bridge they dismounted, Juggler helping Garis. One by one they led the horses off the road. Dianor, going last, pushed the shrubbery back upright, and shored it with a tangle of sticks and last year's leaves.

At the ford they mounted again, and rode into the water. The horses whinnied in protest, and Juggler's stood still, trying to pull her head free of the bit and Juggler's control, and start for shore. Dianor kept Emerald going, and the other two horses after a moment heaved long breaths, as if sighing, and followed after.

The going was fairly easy. The bottom was stony, and so the water carried little dirt. It ran clear and transparent, rippling over the darkness of the stones. They could see where they were stepping, avoiding slippery patches of vegetation, and ready when they came to the deep spots, where the horses had to swim. Dianor's riding skirt floated up when the water was that deep, and flopped on the surface, spooking the horses each time it happened, no matter how often it happened. The horses objected, too, to schools of minnows flitting past their feet, taking the sudden little motions about them for danger. But they responded each time to soothing endearments, and so it was no more than a nuisance.

"What do they think's coming at them, pikefish with teeth?" complained Juggler, the third time, when he had just escaped being thrown.

"Ghosts, maybe," said Dianor.

The air was growing warmer as the sun rose higher. The new leaves were out on the trees by the water, and they were thick enough to shade the stream. Their way was lit by a green-gold light that came from all directions, and reflected the ripples of the stream back up at them, so that they looked as if they rode under the water, instead of over it. The Gillybranch wound dizzyingly back and forth, multiplying the distance to the Longwater. At intervals they stopped and dabbled drops of the dark green-gold water on their eyes to keep from dozing off in the lazy light. If there had been a choice of ways, they thought they could have lost themselves, but the stream, no matter how it turned and doubled, had nowhere to go but the river. The horses' hooves, beating a slow rhythm over stone and sand, were muffled by the water and sounded far away.

Around midmorning they came to the Willowbind Falls. Here the woods thinned, giving way to a water meadow and glades of smaller trees—alders, dogwoods, osiers, willows bending branches in their faces, soft with grey, furry buds. When they were close enough to hear the falls, the horses grew skittish again, frightened by the unfamiliar sound and by the pull of the water as it sped into a narrower channel of rock, heading straight for the Willowbind. This time the horses were relieved to find that the humans agreed with them in their anxiety, and pulled to a halt, looking about them for a place where the banks were low enough to let them scramble out of the Branch. One bank was high and the other too marshy where they were, and they did not want to try the swift waters just above the Willowbind, so they plodded upstream again until a curve left one bank lower than the other, and solid enough to take their weight.

The horses snorted as they stepped out on dry ground and stamped their hooves, apparently glad to have the sound of their own going properly close to foot again, and to feel the wind beginning to dry their legs. Drops of water falling from them caught the light and sparkled in miniature rainbows over the ground.

They rode downstream again over the long grass in the meadow by the creek, and then over rock as they drew nearer to the Falls. There was little soil or grass there, and no trees, except a single, scrubby willow. It was old and stubborn, although it would never be able to grow tall, growing at a tilt out of a crack in the rock at the very edge of the cliff where the water went over. It was blighted on the side facing the water, with the steady pressure of the spray beating it back, but the side facing them was furry with new buds.

Dianor dropped Emerald's reins to the ground, a position which the mare had been trained to think was as good as being tied. Drawn by the thunder of the water, Dianor walked carefully to the cliff edge and lay down by the willow, gripping a handful of thin branches to steady herself. She stared over the edge at the length of white water pouring itself over and down, so loud that it was felt in the bones of the whole body, not heard.

"Dianor!" shouted Garis, but he could not be heard over the Willowbind. He did not want to bring the full weight of a horse any closer to the edge, and could not dismount and go closer himself without assistance. He leaned over to speak into Juggler's ear. "Get her back. She could fall."

Dianor, absorbed in the Willowbind, did not bother to look at them.

Juggler shook his head. "You're not her nurse," he said.

Garis grunted impatiently, but changed his advice. "Go sit on her feet."

Juggler might have obeyed, but by then Dianor had backed off, climbed to her feet, and was running to them, her face wet and her eyes shining. "It's beautiful," she said, shouting it loud enough to be heard.

Garis nodded, and they were silent a while, listening and looking. At last Garis shook his head and pointed along the curve of the cliff. It made a cauldron around the Falls, the rim sloping down a little on both sides. They were on what would be the upstream side when they reached the Longwater. The view was blocked where trees began to grow again, but there did not seem to be any direct way to get to the lower ground, where the Gillybranch completed its descent to the river, unless they were to plunge over the Falls themselves.

They rode slowly along the cliff, drawing north, away from the edge of the cauldron. The sides of the cauldron grew less steep, sloping a little more gently down into the river valley, but still falling away too quickly for them to ride, or even walk, down that way.

Once in the shelter of the trees, they stopped. The roar dropped to a whisper, although they could still see the Falls, and beneath it the bottom of the cauldron and the spray rising up from it. Opposite them, the other side of the rim curved round, faint rainbow colors glimmering along the face of the wet rock where sunlight was reflected. If they rode back around the rim and crossed the stream to the other side of the cauldron, the descent to it would be just as unpromising.

"What do you think, Juggler?" said Garis. "Can we find a way down?"

"I think it's all cliffs from here to the river. If we get over on the other side and follow the river south there are some valleys that slope down, but it's a long way around, and they're probably guarded."

"There must be a valley north at the merchants' town," said Dianor.

"Not exactly," said Juggler. "They built along a cleft there. They call it steps, but boatmen call it the gangway."

"We can't go there," said Garis. "No charter to pass us through." He looked uneasily at the cauldron. "We'll have to climb down, I think."

"Dangerous," said Dianor.

Juggler snorted. "Putting it mildly," he said.

Garis rubbed his hand along his crutch, and tried putting a little weight on the injured foot by leaning into the stirrup, but had to give it up. "See any other way?"

Juggler, looking annoyed, said, "No." He added. "But not here. We'll cut over to the river. The cliff there won't be as sheer as the drop-off by the Willowbind, and there'll be trees growing along the face."

Garis nodded and pulled his gaze away from the cauldron.

"What about the horses?" said Dianor.

"You can lead the other two home with you, can't you?" said Garis.

"I'm not going—" She stopped. "Oh, I suppose I am. Yes, I can lead them." She looked back at the Willowbind and down to where the lower stream would be winding away from it, if they could have seen it. "If I tried the cliff there wouldn't be time for me to get back tonight, and I said I would, so...." She stopped again, looking sour, and reached behind to open one of her saddlebags. She took out a coil of rope.

"No, please," said Garis.

She looked surprised. "You'll need it."

He could not deny that rope would be useful going down the cliff, and was silent.

"But not just yet," said Juggler, diplomatically.

She nodded and set the rope on top of her saddle. Emerald made a little noise, and twisted her head around to see what was going on, but finding nothing alarming in rope, was calm again.

They rode slowly through the trees until they came again to a cliff edge. Dismounting, they walked close enough to look over, and found themselves at the top of a vertical forest, filling the span from clifftop down into the valley of the Longwater. Here the trees had come fully into leaf, and seen from above the treetops looked like giant flowers. The river, far below, looked dark and narrow, marked against the flat bottom.

The ground had a layer of soil against the cliff-stone, and, in consequence, a layer of mud. They remained standing to eat the food Dianor had brought from the inn. As they had arrived late and left early, they were not seeing the inn's best. Their lunch was dried apples, some kind of dried meat, too stale and tough to identify, yesterday's bread, and wedges of four kinds of cheese. The cheeses, however, did credit to the inn, and the horses approved of the oats they were served.

Despite the meal's shortcomings, they lingered over it as long as they could. When the food was gone, Dianor took out the coil of rope again. She handed it to Juggler, but looked at Garis until she caught his eye.

"Thank you, my lady," he mumbled.

"I can see you don't like to take favors," she said, "but one more thing—what about money?"

His face cleared at something he could refuse without having to consult his conscience. "You don't have Melibos coins about you, surely?"

"No." She checked her bags anyway. "No."

Juggler helped Garis slide the crutch inside his tunic, down the back, so that it was held securely by the fabric, and as much out of the way as was possible.

Dianor took out leading reins to fasten on the other horses. "Good luck to you in Melibos," she said, "and a good spring."

"Dianor," said Garis.

"Yes?" she said, turning to him.

They looked at each other as he hesitated, looking for words and not finding them. "I wish you a good year," he said, for lack of better.

Juggler decided to take advantage of added years, and kissed Dianor on the cheek as a farewell. She clung to him for a moment and then let go.

With Juggler's help, Garis looped the rope around the tree nearest the edge and large enough to hold their weight. Garis took both strands of the rope in his hands and legs, dropped over the edge, and began shinnying down.

Garis had reached the perch of a well-rooted tree growing high on the cliff-face, and he was holding the rope steady. Juggler took the strands and scrabbled over the edge. When he reached Garis, they pulled the rope down, looped it, and started the process over.

Dianor watched them until the treetops under her feet hid them from her. She gathered the horses and rode away.

Chapter 5
The Wood Beyond the River

Juggler was never able to form a coherent recollection of the scramble down the cliff. The rope kept snagging in the topmost branches of the trees below them. The branches were too thin to hold their weight, but too tough to break without fraying the rope. Perched together at the base of a tree trunk, the one in front squashing the one behind against the scratchy sandstone of the cliff face, they would waggle and tug at the line, as if trying to land a pike, until it was as far down as it would go on its own. Then one would go down it and take it further yet, if that seemed possible without tearing at it too much, and steady it for the other to follow after. Little by little, they squeezed and scratched their way along.

Crawling down the stone, they dug in with fingers and toes and put as much of the weight on themselves as they could, to save the rope. Garis could not use the injured foot to rest on, and had to go even more slowly and cautiously than Juggler did, as they threaded themselves down between the branches. The crutch became an impossible burden. When they came to a maple old enough to jut further out than the others, Juggler eased the crutch out from where it was snagged in Garis's tunic, shoved it out along a maple branch, and let it drop. It fell to the narrow strip of land between river and cliffside far below them.

Each time they came to a tree rooted strongly enough to the cliff to hold them, they rested, taking turns at being the one inside, pinned against the cliff, and waited until cramped muscles in hands and feet eased enough to let them go on. Bits of sandstone broke off around them, and grains of the stuff worked their way into hair, ears, nose, and mouth. A miniature cloud of sandstone dust and bits of bark puffed out of their clothes at each movement. Their stops to rest grew longer and still longer, and yet were not long enough. They kept going.

Once, a young poplar tree, which they should not have trusted, except that it grew by itself and was the only one they had been able to reach, pulled loose above them. Juggler, steadying the rope, had one foot braced against the sandstone, and one on the trunk of a maple that looked big enough for another resting place, if they could just get themselves perched on it. As the poplar shifted, he fell and found himself sitting astride the trunk, painfully bruised.

Garis landed on top of him, yelling "Let go!" It seemed to take forever for Juggler to think past the pain clearly enough to work out that this was not nonsense, and to let go his hold of one side of the rope. The loop over the poplar came free, and the tree went crashing past them. They found later that they had scratches where the roots had gone by.

It had taken them, after all, only half a second to save themselves and their line, but the memory, the only clear fragment of the descent in Juggler's mind, insisted that it had been hours. They heard the tree lodge beneath them, somewhere along the cliff, caught among other trees, but they did not see it again as they descended. It had gone to one side, or they had gone to one side, or they were too tired to notice it, they were not sure which. They kept going.

Then there was something rocky and flat beneath their feet. They were at the base of the cliff. A narrow ledge separated them from the dark water rushing by.

They stretched out on the rocky ledge, too tired to care about the lumpiness of the rock, and lay still for an hour or so, not asleep, but not awake. It was the taste of stone in their mouths that finally started them moving again. They crawled along the ledge until they located Garis's crutch. Juggler lodged it down the back of Garis's tunic again, and they went on crawling until they came to a spot that dipped low enough to let them reach the water.

They scooped it up to wash their mouths, and then to drink, and then to wash their faces. It was cold. It was sweet as honey to their dry mouths.

They rinsed out sandstone grit, spat, rinsed again, spat, and then drank and drank until their bellies protested.

A boat, sitting low in the water with a weight of goods to trade, came slowly upriver, its coming announced even before it cleared the bend below them by the beat of the drum, marking time for the rowers.

Before it came in sight, they shrank back against the cliff, lying flat along the ledge in shadow, and did not move until it had passed them by, and was out of sight again.

"Think they saw us?" said Juggler.

"No. They were on the other side still—probably sold the best of their goods already in Melibos." Garis stared across the river. "Can you talk like a Melibos?" he asked suddenly, turning to look at Juggler.

"Not convincingly."

Garis nodded, not surprised. "Best keep your mouth shut, then."

Downriver to the south the river made a curve into the east. The Melibos tradesmen had a guild-town of their own in the hollow of that curve. The cliffs were not so high there, and it was an easy road up into Melibos, with a gentler slope, pleasanter for a trader weighted down with packs, than at its counterpart up the gangway through the merchants' town in Emmering, at the corresponding curve of the river.

Garis stopped looking across the river and considered the water at his feet. He leaned over, dabbling at the water and letting it dribble over the scratches on his hands. "We were trying to go the short way round," he said after a time. "There's a little gap where the Pigseye joins the river, and if the Pigseye water's running low you can get across and not have to go all that way east to the bridge—and we took a tumble. We're hands from Glamdill, out of service and going to visit our families who herd, southingward."

Juggler raised his eyebrows. Garis's voice had changed. He was drawling, his voice drifting on the long sounds. It was the Melibos accent. He slowed even more over the names of places beyond the river.

"And you caught cold in your throat and can't talk," Garis finished with Emmering speed. "So now all we need is a good-sized log." He thought a moment. "Two logs," he said. "Where's that winter-born twig-stack tried to bring us down?" He rubbed at a scratch, then realized he was making it worse and clenched his hands to make himself stop.

"Fell on the downstream side, I think," Juggler said, at a guess. His muscles tightened with the fear of falling that the idea of that particular tree brought back to him. He took a deep breath and waited a moment or two for his arms and legs to relax.

Garis nodded, and thought about getting up to walk, then shook his head. They would be too conspicuous if another barge came by.

They picked their way crab-wise along the ledge, peering up at the roots of the nearest trees for one that they might be able to bring down, and into the river for the poplar that had come down past them, or any trunk that might have fallen of itself and lodged in the backwater. Looking without falling off themselves made for slow going.

At last the bank widened a little, and beyond the widest point were rocks, tall enough to show their points, showing even over the springtide surface. Caught among them was an old yellow birch, frilly with curls of bark standing out in the ripple of the current. The poplar tree had snagged against it, branches caught in branches.

"Should do," said Juggler, and Garis nodded agreement.

They worked the pair loose, with Garis holding the water-end of the birch, where it held the poplar. He yelped as the birch came free and pulled him into the river. Juggler shoved at the rest of the trunk, and gritted his teeth to keep from crying out himself as he jumped into the cold waters of the river to get his hold back before their transport got away from him.

They roped the birch and poplar together, making a sort of boat for themselves, although it was not enough of one to keep them out of the water's reach. They lay stretched out flat, Juggler on the smaller tree, the poplar, and Garis on the birch, gripping with their knees and paddling with their hands.

Juggler tried breaking off a branch and sitting up to paddle, but it was not a success. The shifting balance threatened to swamp them, and the twigs did not make enough of a paddle to improve their speed.

After some practice and some duckings that left them numb with cold, they managed to head their brace of trees cross-current without being rolled over by every wave that came along, and without getting their mouths and noses full of river water. Once they came out of the shadow of the cliff, it was a little warmer.

Juggler tried to sing, to set a pace, but he kept getting water in his mouth and then it would go down the wrong way, so he was too busy coughing. He gave it up, and concentrated on the cliffs ahead. Most of their progress was downstream, but slowly the other side was nearing.

They stopped paddling as they drifted by the trade town. There was more boat traffic there, but they tried to look like bumps on a pair of tangled logs, and evidently succeeded. If anyone had been near enough to see that the two trees were not just tangled together, but roped, it could have meant trouble for them, but trees adrift in the water were common enough, and water-logged wood did not have many uses. No one would come out after them to try to salvage the logs.

They came to land, finally, a couple of miles below the Melibos trade town. The ground was still low there. It was not much of a scramble for Juggler, but Garis's crutch, catching in the mud, poked around at odd angles, so they stowed it under his tunic again and with Juggler's help he made the climb up the bank and onto the flat. Juggler retrieved the rope and followed Garis up the bank. They found themselves in a grazing meadow, and at sound of the baaing sheep they finished the scramble slowly and carefully. They managed to get onto the grass without getting onto any droppings.

At sight of them, the flock came meandering over to find out what was happening, if anything. They were big, heavy with the winter's fleece, and bleating their fascination with something different.

Behind them came their dog, barking annoyance at silly sheep who might drown themselves in some fit of absent-mindedness. Juggler pulled the crutch out of Garis's tunic, and Garis tucked it under his arm. Then they allowed themselves to be herded back to the shepherdess, an old woman sitting huddled in the shelter of her long cloak, and only her eyes alive to everything that moved across the meadow.

Garis started to tell her his story, but the herder cut him off after the first few words. "Don't bother me, child, I'm busy." She spared them a glance long enough to consider their bedraggled state. "I can't spare a cloak—River!" That was the dog, it seemed, not the actual water. The dog circled back and nudged a straggling ewe further from the bank. "—but there's bread and curds in my pack," she went on. "Take some if you like."

Garis thanked her, and Juggler opened the leather bag at her feet. He took out the loaf and tore it jaggedly in half, putting one half back again, and tearing the other half into two quarters. Then he took a smaller bag from the bag, and scooped a handful of curds from it and smeared them over the quarter-loaves. Garis offered her his explanation of who they were. Listening to his drawling speech, she nodded, accepting him obviously from their side of the river, not caring about details which were, after all, not as important as sheep. She waved them away, impatiently. Garis repeated hastily, "Many thanks," and Juggler blew her a kiss as they set off.

Eating as they walked, he and Garis squelched across the meadow. At the end a steep path led up out of the valley. They sat down long enough to finish the bread, and then plodded up, stopping at intervals to rest.

The wind had seemed bitterly cold against them at first, but as their clothes dried on their backs, and the food warmed their bellies, it began to seem like a gentle breeze. It smelled of long grasses.

By the time they reached the top, they were dry, except for a little dampness left in their shoes. They had to pause at intervals to scrape off the layers of mud that gathered on their feet and weighted their steps.

"So far, so good," said Juggler. He straightened up from uncaking the current load of mud and looked back over his shoulder at the unmoving shepherdess and the river beyond her. "I wouldn't have thought it'd be this easy."

"Easy?" said Garis. He lowered himself to the ground for another rest.

Beside them, edging the path, was a windbreak of poplar trees, silver branches pointing to the sky. On the other side of the path was another pasture. It was empty as far as they could see, but fresh droppings and the cropped grass showed that it was not abandoned.

"Why aren't there any guards or watchmen or what-not?" said Juggler.

"Probably up at the town or on the bigger crossroads," said Garis. "Wyrond doesn't like to spend money patrolling." He frowned and gave Juggler a look, half amused and half stern. "You have no voice. You have a cold in your throat. Keep in practice for it, if you want to remember it."

"Don't remind me. It's probably going to come true," Juggler said, but after that he was silent. The next question he wanted to ask he asked by pointing across the field, and drawing and sheathing an imaginary sword, to suggest that they could avoid guards if they went off the roads.

"I don't think so," Garis answered. "Next shepherd'd be more inquisitive. There aren't as many guards as you'd find across the river, and they're not as quick to worry, but fewer and slower isn't the same as none at all. We can't afford to look suspicious, or be taken up as trespassers. We're stuck with the roads." He looked at the sun. It was getting low. Juggler helped him up, and they walked on. In spite of Garis's lame foot, they made fair time.

Towards nightfall, on the outskirts of the trade town, they ran into the guards Garis had expected, one on each side of the road, who stepped into the center and called them to a halt, demanding their business. One of them, after listening to Garis's story, tested Juggler's dumbness by stepping heavily on his foot.

As Juggler had half expected something of the sort, his response was an insulted, but voiceless grunt.

The other asked Garis how they came to be out of service. Garis answered readily enough, with the quiet stretch of the words that marked speech in Melibos. Their master had done poorly the year before and then spent more in the winter than he should. Casting new accounts, he decided he was in danger of losing all his land, and would have to try for less in the year ahead, letting some of his workers go, and leaving the fields the rest could not tend to lie fallow. They thought they might have better luck elsewhere.

The guards passed them on. "Sorry," said the one who had tested Juggler, although he did not sound particularly sorry.

Inside the town they managed to find work helping out in the kitchen of one of the inns. It was fortunate that there were several inns to ask at, because with one lame and one officially mute it was not easy to find things they could do that an innkeeper could reasonably consider worth the expense of having them.

They were taken on at one where the innkeeper and his family, like most of the townsfolk, traded in a small way. In consequence, the kitchen work, in addition to the more obvious washing and fetch-and-carry, included going over the count of spices and fine cloth bought, sold, or stacked in the basement. Getting the tallies to match was boring, and took time. The inn's accounts were considerably behind.

It was still not quite done when the innkeeper gave up on it for the night. They had come close to matching, and the mistakes almost balanced. There was too much bitter-hot on hand in the spices, and not quite enough crimson velvet in the rolls of cloths, but it was obvious to him that the problem was mistakes to find somewhere, and not a question of theft. With a sigh and a shrug, he took them back upstairs to the kitchen, and gave them a half-silver each as they sat down to the family's late supper of bread and what was left of a batch of mutton-neck stew.

The bargain had officially been only supper and the night's lodging, and a little more food to see them along the road, but he was impressed that the tallies had come as close to matching as they had.

The next day they were able to get a ride on a wagon going east with a load of winter wheat that had come up with a trader from the south. This took them as far as the Overwood, where the road began to rise. Some rain had fallen in the night, and the driver expected he would be meeting muddy stretches. A passenger who could not get out for those and push was more than he could ask of the horse, not on an uphill road. It was just as well, as it saved them the trouble of finding a good reason to get out in the middle of the Overwood, when they were supposed to be going beyond it to the main road south.

They followed along the road at first, heading east. Ahead of them, the wagon grew small, and then vanished around a bend.

The driver looked back and waved goodbye before the turning hid them from each other.

The mud was not thick, except in patches, and the patches did not fill the roadway. The wagon had not been able to keep out of the mud, but on foot they could manage easily enough, except that it was slow going.

Garis was not sure where they should turn off, and he kept stopping and looking into the wood to the south of them, trying to peer through the thickets, although he thought they needed to be at least a little further along.

For a while, the road was easy to follow. The edges along the road had been cut for timber or charcoal, and the ground was thick with shrubs. About the time their food gave out, they came to where the shrubs had been growing back long enough to make a heavy shade, even without their full growth of leaves. They walked in darkness.

"Doesn't this wizard of yours have a road in?" said Juggler, giving up on his voicelessness as Garis looked fretfully at a break in the shrubs that could have been the start of a path or could be an accident leading nowhere. Juggler whispered the question, not sure if this was for any real fear of being overheard or for fear of the darkness. He cleared his throat to repeat the question in a more cheerful voice, but Garis was answering, also in a whisper.

"I've never heard that anyone could mark a road in here. But he must be somewhere hereabouts."

"But—"

"He keeps wolves to catch mice and watch the bounds, they say. If we try we should be found."

"Or lost," Juggler suggested.

Garis made a face and turned off the road into the break that looked like a path. It soon led them into a tangle of thickets, but not so tangled as to stop them entirely. They made it through with some rips and scratches. Once they were past the vines and bushes, they came to the older, taller trees, and clear footing beneath them, although the light from overhead was almost as dim as in the thickets. The ground was soft and silent with old leaves. They picked off burrs and checked for ticks, although it was early in the year for them to be out, and went on.

Garis had enough woodcraft to spot footprints or droppings, but they did not succeed in finding a trail visible long enough to bring them in sight of a wolf, much less a wizard's house. They felt uneasy without weapons. Knowing that wolves as a rule feared people was not much comfort in the early spring. Food was still winter-scarce, and wolves not in the wizard's service might be hungry enough to try for larger game.

For that matter, who was to say that wolves in the wizard's service would be friendly?

As they trudged through the damp layers of fallen leaves, they kept watching for animals, or signs of animals, and for trees easy to climb. Juggler had to climb every now and again to get a look at the sun and check their direction to be sure they did not go in a circle. And they wanted to be sure they still knew which way the road was, if they had not found a guide to the wizard before hunger forced them to retreat.

Juggler was not much of a climber, but Garis tied a rock into one end of their rope to weight it, and threw it over, and with the rope looped over the first branch, Juggler could scramble up into the branches and then slowly make his way up to the light.

When the darkness thickened into night, they made use of one such tree to sleep in. Garis could not climb, but Juggler drew him up in the rope, and once there they used it to rope themselves to branch and bole. It was safe, but uncomfortable. They ate the last of their food and fell asleep to the whistling of the wind in the branches.

The next day they went yet more slowly. Hunger was telling on them.

They came to a fallen oak branch and sat down on it to rest. There was something odd in the air over it. It took a moment for their eyes to re-adjust so that they could recognize it as a ray of sunlight, coming in through a gap in the leafy crown where the branch had fallen from the tree. The light glimmered in the air, dazzling them.

Garis stood up and thrust his head into the sunbeam. He turned from side to side as if he almost heard something, and even tried snuffing the bright air, as if there was something to smell that would make him more sure of whatever it was he almost felt. "There's something—"

Juggler listened and looked, but could not sense whatever the almost-feeling was that held Garis. "What—?" he said.

Garis scowled at him impatiently for a moment, but then turned, settling on the direction the ray of sunlight pointed. He tried to hurry away along its line, but the tendency of the crutch to sink into the ground at each step made speed impossible. He kept on going as quickly as he could manage, and Juggler followed his lead.

It was not until they came out into a larger patch of light, a clearing in the woods, that Juggler heard the sound Garis had followed. It was an axe striking wood. It sounded dull, not like metal, but more like stone.

At first the light after the dimness was too bright to see by. Then their eyes cleared, and they saw the woodcutter, a girl dressed in a green tunic, with long brown hair hanging down her back in shaggy tangles and bouncing at each blow. The notch into the tree, where the creamy whiteness of the wood gleamed against the bark, grew slowly deeper and wider.

An old man lounged on the grass beside her, watching thoughtfully. His face was as white as his hair and his long robe. "He's mine, you know," he said to the girl.

"That remains...to be seen," she said, timing her words to the intervals of her blows. It seemed as if she would have gone on after the next one to say more, but the old man looked up and saw them. As his eyes met Garis's, she spun around, her axe dropping back to rest on her shoulder.

Garis was already falling, but he was able to look into her face, too, before his eyes closed. He dropped to the ground and lay still.

Juggler tried to cry out, but his throat was too dry. He felt his knees giving way. The ground in the sunlight felt soft and warm, especially after the night in the tree.

They did not wake until the sun had moved far enough to put them back in shadow again. A dead tree now lay stretched on the floor of the glade. There were fresh droppings by it. There was no sign now of the Spring maid with her stone axe or the Winter father watching.

Juggler pulled himself to his feet and at first said nothing, looking carefully at the dead tree in the now empty clearing.

He had seen figures like that woodcutter and her companion before, in the tiles of Dale's palace. He helped Garis up and then broke their silence. "I saw—or dreamt I saw—"

"Spring and Winter?" Garis said. He did not admit to having seen them, too, much less to being troubled by their dispute over which Season claimed one of them as possession, but he could scarcely have known what Juggler's vision was unless he had shared it. And Garis was the obvious choice for the Seasons' arguable claim.

Juggler would have liked to ask more, but Garis's face showed an unwillingness to accept any further questions.

The line of fallen tree and droppings beyond it marked a direction of sorts. They followed it.

The wood continued as before, tall trees shading a soft floor of rotting leaves. Here and there the trees grew more thinly. They caught glimpses of the sun through the trees to the west. The oaks were almost gold, with last year's brown leaves still on the branch and the new leaves not in yet. It was not so much the light itself they saw as the stubborn oak-leaves gleaming with it.

After a while they heard the sound of running water. The trees were not quite as close together as they had been, and they could see some little distance ahead, but they could not see the water. They kept going, guided by the sound of the stream, and after a little they found it. There was a rise in the ground to the east, and the water came rushing out of the earth there, turned south, curving around a trunk unreasonably wide and tall, and then it disappeared, or, at any rate, could not be seen to either side of the monstrous tree.

As they drew nearer, and there were fewer trees between them to block part of what they saw, the big tree suddenly stopped looking like a tree.

It was a tower.

They still could not see what became of the stream from the hill.

There was a door in the base of the tower. Whoever lived inside it apparently did not fear being attacked and the entrance forced. There were no steps leading up to the door. It was set level with the ground, and it stood a little ajar.

They hesitated, each waiting for the other to step forward and try knocking.

The door swung open, and from the shadow within a face leaned out into what was left of the daylight. His hair was black, streaked with red, and his beard was red, streaked with black. His skin was streaked with small white scars from long-healed burns. His eyes were green and bulging.

"Welcome," said the sorcerer Hluvend.

Chapter 6
The Wizard's Tower

Hluvend quietly took charge of them in a way that forbade questions or explanations: set water to heat in a cauldron, brought out goat cheese, hard boiled eggs, and goat's milk, and pumped up cold water into a copper tub. While they ate, he kept an eye on the water over the fire. When it was near boiling, he poured hot water from the cauldron in with the cold in the tub and banked the fire to keep the heated water hot without boiling it away, so that they could go on adding hot to the bath as they liked. He left them briefly, returning with fresh robes.

The robes were too long for Juggler and too large for either of them, but clean warm woolen cloth was too great a comfort to fret over such details. They belted the fabric in for Garis, and up and in for Juggler.

When the food was gone and the baths taken, the wizard took a lamp and led them up a flight of stairs that spiraled up against the wall. The room above was sparsely furnished—two pallets, a chamber pot, and a candlestick. He lit the candle from his lamp. For just a moment the room was warm with the smells of hot oil and hot tallow as the light flared up. He reached up a long arm and tapped at a set of chimes hanging by threads from the ceiling, so that they rang out softly as one touched against another. There was, perhaps, a sort of spell on the chimes' music. It had no tune, but it calmed their thoughts, and soon they found themselves yawning.

"If you need anything, I'm usually at the top," he said. He considered a moment, and looked at Garis's foot. "Something to help against pain, perhaps," he said, and trotted on up the staircase, spiraling out of view into the height of the keep. He was back shortly with two bottles, one small and dark and one larger and clear. He set them down by Garis. "About half of that, if you want it," he said, pointing at the dark bottle. "And water," he added. "You'll want it to get rid of the taste." He pointed at the clear bottle.

"Thank you," said Garis, although by this time the words seemed inadequate to the flow of hospitality. He tried to add something more appropriate in length, but Hluvend had already turned and was on his way up.

Juggler stared after him. "First time I ever met someone who stopped you from getting a word in edgewise in so few words." He stretched and shook his head. "Do you want any of that stuff?" he asked, pointing to the dark bottle.

Garis nodded, beginning to lack words himself, between Hluvend's quiet ways and the sleepy sound of the chimes tapping above them.

Morning came as a bright haze filling the room. When Garis and Juggler woke they could not at first tell where they were, because the even light and the circular wall left them no lines to judge distance.

The chimes hanging from the ceiling flickered a little, but were silent, stirring with the air too gently to come in touch with one another.

The room was lit by long, thin openings, set into the tower like cracks in bark. The shade of the trees around them left no direct window to the sun, but the even brightness that came in through the slits was plenty to see by, once they remembered what there was to be seen.

Garis sat up, blinking, and tried to remember what he had been dreaming, but it was already gone. He turned to Juggler. "Would you go see if Hluvend's awake?"

Juggler started up the stairs, trailing one hand along the railing to be sure of his balance. The banisters were carved as trees, branching to form the rail.

The room above was a library, and above that a workroom. Juggler recognized the tools of weaving, carpentry, and shoe-making, but there were others that he did not know. He saw nothing for smithcraft. Did Hluvend make swords entirely by magic?—probably not, since he had those other, ordinary tools. Juggler concluded that the wizard did not want the weight of forge and anvils on an upper floor. Perhaps there was another room, dug in among the roots.

Hluvend's own room, at the top, was above the trees, and flooded with light in many colors. Instead of the narrow slits he had four windows of colored glass. The one to the east blazed in the morning light. It was a tree with gold trunk, green leaves, and fruit of many kinds. A snake with green and purple scales writhed its way around the edges of the window, biting its tail in the middle of the lower edge.

North was a window mostly of light blue, ending near the top in jagged waves, with clear glass above it. A great ship with scarlet sails was placed, with a cheerful disregard for buoyancy, underneath the waves, in the center of the window. A border of fishes went round the edge, clear glass under water, but flying bright through the air at the top, where each scale was a separate piece of glass, each flying fish gleaming with many colors.

South was a darker window, dim at this hour, although the design of the sleeping colors could still be made out. It showed a green mountain, streaked with red lava, its peak erupting in flames which rose to the very top of the glass and fell down the sides in a border of red and gold sparks.

West was a pane of clear glass with a border of many-colored birds: oriole, jay, cardinal, finch, grackle, and more. Juggler looked round at the windows again, seeing a pattern. "Earth and water," he said quietly, "fire and air."

"Exactly so."

Juggler blinked. In all the colored lights it was hard to distinguish anything solid within the chamber. Then he saw the wizard, reading in bed. "Good morning." Juggler made a bow to his host.

Hluvend nodded, set his book aside, and got up from his pallet. He put on a grey robe over his tunic, stepped into leather slippers, and combed out his hair and beard. "How may I serve you?"

"Would you come talk to Garis?"

The wizard's eyes opened a little wider. "Hmm," he said, too interested by the name to bother answering the question. But the yes was obvious, for he brushed past Juggler and started down the stairs. He paused in the workroom, went to a tall cabinet, and hooking over a stool with one foot, he climbed up and began rummaging among the contents of the top shelves.

In the search he dislodged what were evidently spilled grains of old ingredients. The room was filled with a mixture of herb scents. It was pleasant enough, until a bit of skunk oil was disturbed. Hluvend sneezed, and flapped his hands at the air.

Juggler found some odd cloth-ends on the floor and put one in front of his face to breathe though, passing another up to the wizard, so that he could protect himself against the worst of it.

"Miserable stuff to work with," Hluvend said, his words muffled a little by the rag. "But I use it in love philters."

"Love philters?"

Hluvend looked offended at his surprise. "That and medicines —those are what most people want of me, most of the time. There are things I can't do—or some that I could, but not without spending more of my time and substance than most people can afford to pay me for. Some I won't do. Take away those, count what's left, and there you are. I make love philters." He added with a sigh, "I can't claim that they're entirely effective —there are limits to what magic can do. But they help a little. And people ask for them." He pulled out a bundle of something weedy, shook his head irritably at yet another item he wasn't looking for, and shoved it back. He rummaged again and pulled out a long box of translucent crystal with something inside it and gave a whistle of relief. He hopped off the stool, slammed the doors of the cabinet, and fled to the staircase, leaving the skunk oil to finish dissipating on its own.

Garis took a deep breath as the two came into sight and launched into his prepared speech. "Sir, I am most grateful—"

Hluvend squatted down beside him and set the crystal box on the floor between them. "So you're the prince of Emmering," he said, looking at Garis with much interest. "Say something."

Garis looked at him, puzzled, and then at the crystal box. It was featureless, without latch or lock or any sign of an opening along any of its sides. "A password for it, you mean? But I don't know of any."

The crystal melted away, and the liquid from it evaporated, leaving a puff of cold air. The thing inside was a sword, made of good iron, without inlay or jewelling. The hilt was wrapped in plain brown leather. The only decoration was the pommel, which was a ball of bone-ivory, polished smooth and glimmering in the light.

"That's Bonefrost," said Garis, not quite asking.

"Oh, yes, that's Bonefrost," said Hluvend. He picked it up and ran his finger down the flat of the blade. He was silent a moment, as if listening, then nodded and handed it to Garis.

Garis took it warily. It looked ordinary enough, and felt so, too, as far as he could tell. He held it in one hand and it seemed to balance well. He did not feel like standing up and swinging it indoors to be sure. He set it down at his side. "It's an antidote to poison, they say," he said, hopefully.

"Yes."

Garis waited, but Hluvend did not add anything. After a moment Garis said, "I thought it might have other powers. In battle. The legends said—"

The wizard looked at him with surprise, and rumpled his beard reaching up to scratch his chin. "Do you need that much encouragement to fight?" said Hluvend.

"No!" Garis spoke angrily, thinking his courage was in question.

"No, I didn't think so," the wizard said. He was silent a moment, considering both Garis and the sword. "Well, it recognized your right to it. You'll find it handles well, but if you aren't used to using one, it won't teach you."

Garis, a bit insulted, said stiffly, "My guardians saw to it that I had training."

Hluvend said, "What about your foot? If you were wondering —no, I can't speed the healing."

"It's better than it was. Might be well enough. But, anyway, I'll be horsed when we start, I think, and I'll try to stay so."

"Yes?" Hluvend considered it. "Yes, perhaps."

"Would you bet on the chances?" Juggler said.

"I don't bet when I don't know the odds," the wizard said crisply.

Garis did not argue. Time was part of the odds now, and he could not wait for more of it nor could he avoid taking the risk. But the odds were perhaps on his side.

Hluvend nodded, lost in thought, combing his beard smooth again with his fingers.

Garis rubbed at his own chin, uneasily. It was scratchy, in the places where his beard grew. It would be starting to look patchy. He went back to his prepared remarks. "Sir, I do not know how I can repay you—"

"For a night's care and giving you back your sword?—send me a gold piece, if you find some, and can find a messenger to leave it somewhere nearby. The wolves will let me know."

"You knew we were coming, then?" Juggler said.

"These are my woods," the wizard replied.

"If you trust me for the payment, I'd like to ask more."

"Yes?" Hluvend chuckled, as Garis rubbed at his chin again. "A razor? I'll hunt one up."

"No, I mean—thank you, yes. But besides that. Can we borrow horses to ride as far as the river and money to try to find passage over?—and I wonder...." Garis trailed off.

Hluvend shook his head. "I don't keep horses," he said flatly. "They don't get on with the wolves. Passage is another matter, though." He closed his eyes for a moment, calculating. "I don't think you want horses and the hire of someone's ferry," he said. "Stealth will serve you better. I'll start you out. Ten golds, and twenty books. The castle must have something of a library."

"It does," said Garis, "but I don't know what's in it."

"I do," said Juggler.

"Good. We'll discuss it later," said the wizard, obviously enjoying the prospect. He thought a moment, and added, "Mind, that's the books themselves, not copies."

"Why?" said Garis.

"Sometimes I can read what other readers thought of the words. Sometimes," he repeated, and looked at the streak of light coming in one of the window slits, evidently losing himself in a memory of other books and the readers before him. "And anyway," he added, "with each scribing errors may be added. Don't let that stop you from getting copies made before you send them to me—just make sure the copiers are careful." Hluvend stood up and stretched. "You should rest and eat today, I think, and leave tomorrow."

Juggler said abruptly, "Sir, do you send illusions to guide people here?"

Hluvend shook his head. "No. You'd been fasting—that brings visions here, sometimes."

He did not seem inclined to elaborate on his answer, and Garis did not seem inclined to ask him to. Juggler gave it up and spent the day helping the wizard with household chores. He had hopes of observing a spell or two being set, but Hluvend took advantage of extra hands to get through the commonplace chores that even wizards must do—and even wizards put off doing—until there are no clean garments in the wardrobe and no food on the shelf. They gathered eggs and deloused the chickens, baked bread, washed clothes and floors, and weeded the garden. They talked of books and how long they took to copy, and which ones Hluvend was to have as payment. Garis helped in the chores which did not require much standing or walking.

The next morning Hluvend brought them outside the tower. Both Garis and Juggler looked doubtful as they found waiting there a simple log boat made of a tree trunk with the inner wood burnt out. It was barely long and wide enough for the two of them to sit one behind the other or lie down side by side, and barely short and narrow enough to go through the hole where the stream vanished underground.

Hluvend's big eyes flashed with amusement as he took in their expressions. "For shipcraft, go to the sea," he remarked. "It floats, and that's about as much as you need. Don't cross the river in a storm or a high wind, and don't look for speed. Look for the other side, and you should find it."

"I don't suppose a spell—" Garis began.

Hluvend shrugged. "It isn't a kind I do. I'm no waterwitch." He bent down and took hold of the boat's side, staring at the line of wood against the water. After a moment, he straightened up, and rubbed his back. "I've asked the wood to keep an eye on you, but of course the heartwood is out of it, and it's the best I can do with it."

"Thank you," Garis said uncertainly.

Hluvend went on without listening, "Some places this time of year the tunnel's full, and you'll have to hold your breaths. Count of thirty is as long as it gets." He seemed to think that this was plenty of reassurance, and that their count to thirty under water would be the same as his. "Couple of drops, couple of feet each, and you may bump walls or columns along the way, but there's nothing you can do about it except brace yourselves. Look out for the crosscurrents at the Longwater."

Garis took a breath, tugged his belt around so that Bonefrost would not be in his way, and handed his crutch to Juggler. Carefully, he lowered himself into the log and stretched out, lying on his side. Juggler put the crutch down in the middle of the log, and wedged himself into the remaining space. Hluvend handed into them their rope and a leather bag with a loaf of fresh bread, and they squirmed about until they had made room for these as well.

Hluvend knelt down to shove them off, grunting at the weight of wood and bodies. For a moment, nothing happened, but then there was a sucking sound beneath them. The mud gave way, and the end of the log which had been on land was in water. The log tilted wildly, and then they were falling down the sinkhole. The wizard had evidently done some building in the shaft. Instead of a vertical plunge, it was a steep slope into the earth. It chuted them into a long, low passage, and the first of the promised duckings. The first one only doused them and brought them into air again. The ones that followed were longer, but the stream was going faster than the wizard reckoned, or his reckoning perhaps took into account people who counted such things too fast. They never had to hold their breaths as long as he had led them to fear. The longest count was 19 by Garis's reckoning and 16 by Juggler's.

It was long enough, however, to leave them gasping, with their hearts pounding, long after the passage opened out and took them into slower water and wider spaces. They drifted through a succession of caves they could not see, but guessed at by the feel of the water and the sound of their voices. Where one cave opened into another the water rushed forward, sometimes filling the opening and ducking them briefly again.

The water was warmer than the river, and grew warmer as they went further down. The water inside the log made their boat feel more like a floating bathtub, except for the rocking, the darkness, and the occasional collisions with unseen pillars of stone.

In one cavern, the ceiling rose high in the center, and a hole far above them let a gleam of sunlight into the darkness. For a few moments, they could see lines of crystal gleaming in bright colors—clear purple, rosy pink, the blue of a winter sky—along the stone columns that tapered like icicles down from the ceiling and grew up wide and rough from the cavern flooring. Then the opening grew lower, and they were in dimness, with the shaft of light behind them, dazzling their eyes as they looked back at it. Then they reached a wall, and the stream gave them another ducking, and when they rose into the air again they could see nothing.

It was night when the stream spilled them out into open air. They were not quite sure if it was the night of the same day they had started or the next. There was no moon. The stars seemed intolerably bright and close, pressing down upon them. They could tell by the way the underground stream had flowed that they were somewhat south of Hluvend's tower, but still far from the southern borders of either Melibos or Emmering. Once the stream entered the river, the Longwater's current as they crossed would take them only a little farther south.

As quickly as they could, they sat up and leaned over, one on each side, to paddle with their hands for shore. They could not land, as the bank was too high, cut through stone, but they slowed themselves considerably before the stream spilled again, taking them into the river itself. The rush of cold water swept them downstream. They paddled against it, and at last Juggler was able to grab hold of a maple-root sticking out over the water. He pulled them in under its shelter next to the bank. The top of the bank was still too high above them for them to get to land, but holding still gave them a chance to catch their breaths, without having to worry about turning over or being swept too far downstream. They could stretch their cramped muscles, and unseal the bag to bring out the food the wizard had given them.

Despite the tight leather covering, their loaf of bread was waterlogged. They were too hungry to grumble at it, and swallowed the mush without a word. By the time they had finished it their eyes had adjusted to the starlight, and the night was properly dark, as night should be.

They could see the water by the streaks of starlight on the waves. Land was visible as solid darkness between the stars and the waves. They were between high bluffs, with the high ground continuing both upriver and down as far as they could see.

Juggler shivered and rested his head against the roots above him. "Dale's supposed to have all the low stretches patrolled," he said.

Garis grunted in agreement.

"I suppose the pass wouldn't have helped," Juggler said wryly. "And anyway, it'd have been wet through, and maybe not up to so much water."

Garis shook his head. "Parchment's tough."

"What about the ink? Would it've still been legible?"

Garis grimaced, acknowledging the point and sat up in the boat, considering the line of the bluffs.

"Any smugglers in your army?" Juggler asked, although he could guess at the answer, or Garis would have planned for help in that way to begin with.

Garis shook his head. "No," he said, "no smugglers. The clever ones get off the river by bribing guards or finding ways in they keep secret, and they don't get caught. The ones who get caught are the foolish ones, and I didn't dare trust them."

Dale and the merchants together had built walls and set guards to close off all the reasonable river landings, except the merchant guildtowns, which were carefully guarded. The landings that had been walled off were not watched as closely. Guards were on duty at only a few of the walls at any one time, but smugglers loaded with goods—or invaders loaded with heavy armor and weapons—would hesitate before trying to scale or breach a wall, knowing that soldiers might be at the top of it, or might show up before they had finished the job.

Garis hesitated, too. He and Juggler did not have much besides themselves to get over a wall, but even that little would take time. He had a good sword, a bad foot, and a long rope. "We'll go up the cliff," he said. He did not need the starlight to know that Juggler was making a sour face, getting sourer as he realized there was no better plan he could offer to Garis.

They shoved off from the bank. This time they did not lie down to let the current take them where it liked. They knelt, one behind the other, so that they could paddle with their hands and give some direction across the current to their little wooden hulk.

The current took them downstream, and they made what speed they could across it to the other side.

The river was as cold going back as it had been coming out, but the log-boat sheltered them from the worst of it. They fetched up on a spit of sand and struggled out of the boat, sinking over their ankles as they tried to stand. Garis knelt and put his hands on the log. "Thank you," he said. "A good journey to you." He shoved it out into the current, and struggled to his feet.

It was getting light.

The log moved further out toward the center of the river, picking up speed as it drew farther away from them. It looked as if it had an aim of its own, but they couldn't tell if it would be to follow the river to the ocean, or to fetch up somewhere on the eastern side of a bend and be found by someone in Melibos who might recognize it as Hluvend's work and bring it home.

They slogged across the wet sand to the narrow strip of dry sand at the foot of the cliff. Above them the maple trees rose in levels, as orderly as a court gathered for a play, although there was only the river for the trees to watch.

Going up was slower than going down, but it was easier to avoid looking down and making themselves giddy. By the time sunlight reached them they were almost a quarter of the way up. They tied themselves to a pair of large trunks and dozed uncomfortably through the day.

The trees here were almost fully in leaf. The clusters of red and gold mapleflowers were gone. They were well hidden from the eyes of any travelers who might pass on the river below or the cliff above, looking in their drab clothes like part of the bark behind the leaves.

At sunset they began to climb again. The moon was almost full, giving plenty of light for them to look for footing, but not enough for other eyes to find them. Halfway through the night they crawled onto flat, silver land beneath the moon. It seemed odd to look forward instead of up, but the moment of dizziness went by, and the rock steadied beneath them.

Chapter 7:
Eldwin's Army

When daylight came, they set out northwest—or west—or north, whichever the trees and the footing made easier—and came near the end of the day to farmed land. They were not sure just where they were, but it did not matter much. They still had to go farther north and farther west, and beyond the wheat was a hedge, clearly following the line of a path that would lead to a village market. While they waited for the sun to finish setting, Garis unsheathed Bonefrost and practiced some lunges and parries. The wizard's claim that the sword was properly balanced and handled well was accurate.

After dark they crept over the field to the path and followed it. No matter what village it led them to, their way was easy now. The road would be their guide to larger roads, and so to the palace. Only a heavy rain, turning the way to mud, could stop them, and the sky was clear.

They passed the first village in darkness, without stopping or trying to find food, in case it was a resting place for border patrols. Now that they were inside Emmering, being stopped by guards would not mean being kept out as intruders. All it could mean was that they would be sent to the king for judgment, and since the king's judgment would presumably involve locking them up in a prison that was largely under Garis's control, there was little danger in capture.

But losing Bonefrost, if they were caught before Garis had a chance to hide it—or even arranging to go back to find it again, if he did manage to hide it—would be inconvenient. So they kept themselves hidden as far as they could manage it, coming out only when hunger urged them to it.

They were hungry enough, they decided, when they reached the second village. Juggler sang for their supper. If his accent marked him as from elsewhere, it was not from Melibos, and he had the tone of someone who had lived a fair time in Emmering.

Garis had some little trouble picking up the right speed again. He stayed quiet, listening to a farmer's girl and a trader haggling, until he was sure of his tongue.

At first they were too hungry to make much speed. They had to stop for rest often. The days, and even the nights, were warmer than they had been. They could sleep out in the open without much discomfort. They could barter fewer hours of their work for food and the chance to clean themselves enough to look presentable, instead of spending a good part of the day working long enough to have lodging made part of the bargain. In consequence, they made better speed. The story they told now was that they were going to the castle hoping to find work.

Garis was disappointed to hear praise of the king. As they were off the main roads, the people they met had seen little of the patrols, and their movements had not been so closely watched as in more travelled parts. The older folk talked of the fairness of the king's taxes—not like the bad old days, when there was the fighting between Dale and old King Garis, and everyone laid claim to everything.

The younger folk said that might be, but the taxes could be lower if the king put his mind to it. The elders shrugged their shoulders.

Garis listened and said nothing, except at intervals to remark that there was a good deal in whatever it was the speaker was saying, a procedure that usually led to still further opinions, and a general conviction that the attentive young listener was a good boy. Juggler tended to daydream, letting Garis's good manners carry them both along.

They toiled along in this way for a couple of days, making fair speed, although Garis's foot was still weak enough for him to continue using his crutch. Then about mid-morning they heard wheels behind them and looked back to see a wagon overtaking them. They pressed up against the hedgerow to give it room, but as it came by, Garis said, "Hey! Stop!"

The old man driving the team reined in and looked them over, rubbing absently at the calluses on his hands. He did not seem to approve of what he saw.

"I know you, don't I?" said Garis. He pointed at the bunch of purple clover blossoms painted on the side of the wagon. "You work for Lady Eldwin, don't you?"

"I might," he said cautiously. He frowned, thinking about it, and the wrinkles on his forehead and around his mouth deepened into lines as sharp and complicated as a spider's web, oddly at variance with the smoothness of his bald scalp.

"I'm Garis—maybe you've seen me with my lady, or heard her mention me?"

"I might," the driver agreed again.

"I don't remember your name, but I've seen you—you go out buying goods for my lady, I think."

"Might think that without knowing any ladies," the old man said, jerking his thumb toward the heap of leather hides in the wagon. But his look softened, and his face smoothed into less complicated lines as he added, "They call me Vervin, mostly. I don't suppose I mind if you ride along." He considered Garis carefully once more, then, apparently satisfied with that much, looked at Juggler and back to Garis by way of question.

"Yes, please. Both," said Garis.

Vervin sniffed, which they took for permission to climb in. The hides filled most of the space, but at each corner there was some room left over. They wedged themselves down, and Vervin clucked to the horses.

It was an uncomfortable ride, bouncing over every bump or sag or pebble in the road, but it was better than walking. They even fell asleep for several hours, leaning forward to pillow their heads on the hard leather.

Vervin never actually admitted to acquaintance with Garis, but he passed back a share of his bread and cheese and dried turnips, and a bottle of smallbeer to wash them down. When twilight came he did not look for anywhere to stay, but only pulled in, at a wide spot in the road, long enough to give the horses some rest and a chance to eat grass at the side of the road, and to let the humans stretch a bit and relieve themselves.

"You a mind to keep an eye on the road?" he asked Garis, when the horses were satisfied.

"If you let me."

Vervin climbed into the back of the wagon and rolled himself into one of the hides. After a moment's thought he nodded at Juggler to take another for himself. Garis told the team to get-up, and they drove on beneath the round moon. Vervin sat up stiffly at first, his bald scalp catching the light and looking like a second little moon, floating in air, to all appearances, over the darkness of the leather hide.

The horses plodded on, and at length Vervin seemed to feel sure that Garis was neither going to drive into a ditch nor let the horses take fright and bolt. His head fell forward, and he slumped further down into the leather hide so that it shaded him completely. The extra moon vanished, leaving only the one in the sky to keep watch as Garis drove.

Near the turning of the night they came to a shallow stream. Vervin woke and called for another brief halt. The horses took this as their cue to drink some water and munch on the grass growing beside the water. Vervin grunted as he eased himself to the ground. "Night air. Gout," he said, when he came back from the bushes, in the accents of one uttering deep curses.

"Lot of pain?" said Garis. "If you know how far it is to the next village, I could—"

"It'll be night there, too," said Vervin. "No, I'm awake."

Juggler started to offer to drive, but Vervin blew his nose and hoisted himself onto the driver's seat. "Come up, then," he said, and they climbed into the back again.

It was hard to sleep in the brightness of the moonshine. Garis and Juggler dozed and waked and dozed again as Vervin drove them through the night, with the wagonload of hides.

Some time after moonset he must have started to push the team, because when the dawnlight brightened enough to wake them fully, they saw that they had come farther than they had expected from their reckoning of the distance. They were on familiar ground, rolling up the Southroad and close to Lady Eldwin's holding. Before the sun could rise and show them clearly to any early-goers on the way, they had reached the front wall of her grounds and driven the wagon through the gate.

Inside there was a considerable bustle going on, of field workers getting up and ready to begin. The stirring was perhaps too much for the work. Eldwin's fields were wide, but even so the number of workers was too large. Certainly they could not all be her regular servants.

Vervin drove to the front door and pounded on it. "Leather," he announced to the youngster who opened it. "And them." He nodded at his passengers, unhitched the team, and led them off to the stables, leaving it to the girl to wake up and decide what to do with a wagonload of leather hides and how to welcome the guests whose rank, if any, he did not choose to admit to recognizing.

Her way of handling them was to leave them on the steps while she went in search of stronger arms for unloading the wagon and wiser heads for making decisions. One of her choices, happily, was Breredon the steward, who came so promptly that he still had a bundle of clean linen in his arms. He raised his eyebrows at the new arrivals, and worked a hand free from the sheets to pat the youngster's shoulder approvingly.

She curtseyed, and left them.

"Hello, Breredon," said Garis.

"Good morning, sirs," Breredon answered, sweeping them in with a haste that did not match the casual tone of his words. Jittering up and down on his toes, he led them to the quiet chamber where Eldwin had received them before. He took a moment to still himself, informed them that his lady would be told of their arrival, and glided primly away.

Soon Eldwin came running, barefoot and capless, her hair in a long braid down her back. "I'm glad you're back, my dear," she said to Garis. She embraced him, winced at the roughness of his stubbled face, and embraced Juggler more carefully, although his beard was long enough to be soft, only looking rough because it was tangled and dusty. She looked at Garis again, concerned to see him using a crutch to walk.

"I can ride," he told her. Trying for cheerfulness, he added, "I see you have my army ready."

"I have your army. I don't know if they're ready," she said. "Many of them were a long time on works levied by the king's guards. Those have been badly run. They'll follow you, I expect, but I don't know if they'll fight. No spirit, no strength, and not much trust in anyone."

"It hardly matters," said Garis.

"No," she agreed ruefully. The "army" within the dungeon would matter more in taking the castle than the assault from outside.

Garis's stomach growled, startling them, and he laughed, a little awkwardly, not really amused at the rude sound it made.

Eldwin started to call for Breredon, but the steward was just on his way in again, his burden of sheets disposed of, and replaced by a tray of milk and porridge.

Something in the lift of an eyebrow suggested that Breredon would have preferred to recommend that they wash first, and had given way to letting hunger come first over the protests of his conscience.

Garis chuckled, and said, "Thanks," with a little extra emphasis as he took his porridge.

"It's as well you're here," said Eldwin. "It's one thing to call in all one's debts, but it's another to feed the gang. They're eating me out of house and field, and there's no honey left, if you were wondering."

Breredon vanished with the empty tray.

"I'm not complaining," said Garis, digging into his bowl with relish.

Eldwin nodded at the sword. "I see you found it."

"Yes."

An orange cat wandered into the room and decided that Juggler smelled of many interesting places. It sniffed him up and down, then settled at his side on the cushion and plopped over on its back, with the air of one who would be greatly astonished if not petted. Juggler obliged.

Meanwhile, Garis was asking Eldwin how much they had to equip their army.

"Little enough," she said. "I wasn't able to buy much iron —Norcote keeps an eye on the metal-workers. I have a few mailshirts, and spear-heads ready to put on staves. Some axe-heads, too. Not much in the way of swords or maces. Buying those can be touchy. I've been getting in a good stock of leather, though—"

"We noticed," said Garis.

"—and most of it's been made up into caps and tunics. There'll be that much protection for most of them." She thought a moment. "No, all of them, now," she added, remembering Vervin's arrival. She eyed the sword beside Garis. "And there's that, of course," she said quietly.

He handed it to her. As Garis had done himself, she tested its swing and balance, and her face lightened as she felt the iron cut the air.

"That should be useful," she commented, handing the sword back to him.

"Does Norcote know you've been buying leather?" Garis asked, putting the sword down again.

She spread out her hands. "Probably. But you can't really arrest people for buying leather. At any rate, he hasn't. So far. Afraid the other nobles would bellow—I hope. Anyhow, leather is useful for plenty of things. I made no secret of buying up the forced-labor gangs for extra planting, and it's no surprise to anyone if I want to put them into something that wears well."

"Not everyone does it," said Garis.

"Not without pressure from court, and there hasn't been much of that. But ragged workers don't work as well, so it's not so very suspicious, in itself, if I bother to do it. Still, I was beginning to wonder who would knock at my door first. Fortunately, I see with much relief, it's you."

"We'll hope it's fortunate," said Garis.

"If the year grants it," she said. "And by the way, your wizard's gear is all very well, but I have something for you, too." She got up, shivering as her feet touched the floor, and went from the room, leaving them to their breakfast. She returned shortly, arrayed in a more seemly fashion, with her hair coiled under a grey cap and slippers on her feet. She still wore a plain grey robe, but had added a necklace and belt of purple embroidered work, and she carried on each hand a shield of wood covered by layers of leather, and a third under one arm.

Neither shield was surprising. One was painted with Eldwin's sign—purple-headed clovers scattered on a silver field. The other had the sign of the kings of Emmering, without the waves Dale had added—just a row of gold wheat-stalks on green. The third was painted plain green. But Garis's smile suddenly faded, and he caught his breath.

Juggler and Eldwin both looked at him in surprise. The sight of Eldwin's fresh-painted shield, and the gift of good shields for his own use and for Juggler's did not seem reasonable cause for concern.

"I hope you don't plan to try to talk me out of fighting," she said, not sure what to make of his discomfort.

"Do me any good?" he asked.

"No."

He sighed. "I'd like to be sure I have your advice to come back to. But others will fight for me if they see you there. So I need your sword—or would it be a spear?"

"I've kept one of the swords for myself."

"Good," he said, but he still sounded ill at ease.

"Garis, you're not still fretting, are you, because you have to lead the troops outside instead of staying with the real work inside—"

He shook his head. "My foot won't do for much running on, so I have to ride. And I have to be seen, even if that means going where the danger isn't."

Eldwin frowned. "There's plenty of danger to go around. You aren't planning some glorious stupidity like being first through the gates?"

He snorted. "No, I'll wait till the murder-hole is stopped up."

"Then what is it?—if you're worrying about feeling afraid, that's to be expected before—"

He shook his head impatiently. "That isn't it."

"Well?" she said.

"I feel ... I don't know." He stopped and shook his head, trying to find words.

A puff of chill air, like the breath of Winter, stirred in the room.

Garis rubbed his hands together. "I feel too cool," he said.

"You need a better cloak," Eldwin said wryly. "I'll have Breredon find you one."

"No, not cold!" he said. Then he saw that she was beginning to understand, and added, "Well, I wouldn't say no to the cloak." He was still rubbing his hands together. "But I meant— The rest will be in more danger, and that doesn't bother me now. And *that* bothers me. If I don't care about them, I don't think I like myself very much."

Eldwin considered this malady. "I'd advise a bath—and a shave—and a nap."

Garis nodded, without looking much comforted.

Lady Eldwin suddenly realized that she had been entirely ignoring a guest, and turned hastily to Juggler. "You'll want to get some rest, too, minstrel. I'm not as thoughtless as I seem this morning—I've saved one of the mailshirts for you."

Juggler looked taken aback at this somewhat menacing hospitality. "Thank you," he said.

"Also a room with good beds," she said, and this time she did call Breredon back, to take them away to use them.

The cat looked reproachful as Juggler got to his feet, but when he leaned down to pick it up and carry it along with him, it meowed a protest at being confined and squirmed away.

"Go catch a mouse," Garis told it.

It looked at him even more reproachfully and sat down on the shield of clover.

Juggler spent most of the day dozing.

Garis napped during the rest of the morning, but after the noon dinner he went out into the fields to help with the planting and talk to the workers. This scheme did not work very well, as he could not keep up with them, and they looked at him sideways when he asked questions about themselves, and answered him mostly, "Umm," or "Dunno." He gave it up and worked silently until a rest period was called. Then he tried asking whose beer they thought was best brewed, and what foods gave the most strength. They had worked for most of the land-owners in the kingdom, for pay, or on forced labor and the resulting arguments over food and drink led them on to other matters. Their conversation ran more on the doings and (especially) the mis-doings of the great folk than on themselves, but as Garis was interested in both he was well enough content.

Some of Eldwin's workers were there as forced labor, and the ones who weren't were listed on her records as forced labor, but in fact all of them were getting wages—on the low side, as there were enough of them to be a strain on her budget, but not so low as to produce more than mild grumbling. Some had been thieves or brawlers, but the rest used their numbers to enforce quieter behavior on Eldwin's fields.

At sunset they were brought into the hall to be given supper. Garis slipped away from them and ate with Juggler and Lady Eldwin in private. He was tired, resting his head on one hand even as he ate.

"Are you all right?" Juggler asked him. "I meant to go out halfway through the stint and try to talk you into stopping, but I didn't wake up properly until too late."

"It was interesting," said Garis thoughtfully, and added, with a touch of mockery, "You should have joined us—you won't sleep tonight."

He had not answered Juggler's question, but his face gave a reasonably satisfactory answer. In spite of the weariness that showed there, it was an easy look, without the tight lines of pain that had marked him often during their journey, and he seemed to have forgotten even the coolness that had disturbed him in the morning. He began to repeat some of the more interesting or at least amusing comments he had gathered.

Juggler asked for the pepper and applied himself to his food.

After a little, Eldwin said, "You'll want finer clothes to address them. I had some made ready for you."

Garis chewed thoughtfully on a stewed turnip. After getting it down, he said, "I don't think so, my lady. Let's keep that for tomorrow—afterwards." At the word he looked thoughtful for a moment. There was the possibility of not having an afterwards. Then he went on, "No, I've worked with them now. I'll wear the same for them. But I want you and Juggler by me with the shield and Bonefrost ready to show. Those will be color enough, I think."

Towards the end of the meal, Breredon the steward went out briefly. When he re-appeared, he reported that he had met Dikon outside the palace wall and told him of Garis's return. Dikon sent greetings, he said. At a quizzical look from Garis he added to this formal welcome a fair imitation of a smothered whoop and cheer.

When they went into the hall, a few of the people there were still eating, but silence fell quickly. The forced workers could see as clearly as Lady Eldwin's own servants that she had brought in too many workers for the fields. The fields were wide, but not that wide. It might have been an ostentatious display to impress someone—the king and the court, or the nobles nearby, or far away, or the trade guild—and nothing that would matter to them, but it made them edgy. And now they could see there was an edginess about her ladyship and the servants most in her confidence. The odd new arrival, the boy with the bad foot who had spent the afternoon working with them when he didn't seem to have to, looked like an answer to the puzzle. They eyed him carefully.

"I am Garis, and son of Garis, king of Emmering."

His announcement was greeted with nervous laughter from some, and wary silence from a good many. A few of the forced workers and several of Eldwin's servants tried cheering, but the sound was too weak for the hall, and they gave it up.

Garis raised his head a little higher and his voice a little louder, and went straight on, "Tomorrow I'll ask you to plant a different crop. You'll go with me to the king's castle. We'll be joined there by others—I won't tell you more than that about them now—"

"Because they aren't there!" someone suggested, loudly.

"I don't mind if you don't believe it, Nester," Garis said, scoring a point by having managed to remember the heckler's name. "I just don't want you to repeat it. You'll have spears and—"

He was interrupted by hoots of outrage from the forced workers.

Garis fixed his eyes on Nester, and waited.

Nester took in a breath, thought better of using it, and let it out again. Garis had spent some time that afternoon listening to him complain about the length of the terms of service they put in. Most of the others agreed with him, but they were tired of hearing him talking, as they feared, too much about it, and they would not risk putting themselves in danger by talking themselves. What Garis thought was unclear, but he had listened.

"I also don't mind if you don't fight," said Garis.

"You don't mind!" said someone else. "What makes you think there was any chance of it!"

"A good point," said Garis. "Those of you who serve my lady as her own workers—you'll have to take it up with her if you choose not to fight. I imagine you'll be out of a post. Those of you serving on forced labor—there'll be no one to watch you once the fighting starts. If you run away, that's your business. You'll be as free as any outlaw. If I win, and if you happen to get yourself caught later, I'll double the time you're supposed to be serving. But if you fight for me, I'll cancel any time you have left to serve and give you money to tide you a while till you can find work of your own choosing."

This bought him a moment's silence as they thought it over.

"No posts to offer in your own service?" said Nester.

"Some, I think. I won't know immediately. If I can't give you work, I'll try to help you find it."

There was silence again as they considered the bargain. It was not much to offer. But that very modesty made it sound as if the lame youngster thought he could keep his side of it.

Garis held out his arms to Juggler and Eldwin, reaching carefully so as not to shift his crutch. They gave him sword and shield, iron blade and gold wheat flashing in the torchlight. He held the shield higher. "This picture I suppose you've seen before." Then he flourished the sword with, for a moment, a childish delight in broad motion and brightness. "This is Bonefrost, my father's sword."

The forced workers said nothing, but there was a little hiss of breath, drawn in sharply through the hall at the sword's name. As Eldwin had said, Bonefrost had a reputation. A few of them were old enough to have seen it in action when Garis's father had held it. The rest, like Garis, had heard stories.

Garis talked, then, about what he had seen in Emmering —the fear of Dale and of Lyndred, the fear of war, the wish to travel and trade freely. Dale had brought order, but it was paid for dearly. He wondered to himself if the freedom he hoped to give would be as costly, but he did not dare to say so. If he won the support of the forced workers, that in itself could add to his problems later, for some were violent types, and their townsfolk would not be greatly pleased to see them free to come home. But Garis would have at least one advantage over Dale in trying to ease their fears and balance their claims—he knew them better. If he took care not to cut himself off from them and what they had to tell him, the knowledge could serve all of them.

"None of you has cause to love Norcote," he said, at last. It was a safe guess. Dale had been reigning a long time, and it was bound to have been Dale or judges appointed by him who had sentenced the forced workers. And Eldwin's servants all knew themselves in disfavor with Dale simply by being in service with her. Garis looked quickly around to see if there was someone who wanted to claim loyalty to Dale, and saw that on that point, at least, they were all with him.

Nester was running his hand over his beard, stroking it smooth, and not inclined to offer any look of support. But silence from him was impressive to the rest.

"We'll be leaving an hour before dawn," Garis said. "Stay until the first charge against the wall—I ask that much. Then do as you like." He tightened his hold on Bonefrost and swung it up for them to see, and down again, letting the blade flash in the light. He handed it back to Juggler then, and let the wheat-shield drop into Eldwin's hands. He turned, awkwardly, because of the crutch. He wished he could have done without it, but there was no help for that. He could ride, and he could lead a charge.

The same few who had cheered before cheered as he left. The sound was not so weak this time. Some of the others had joined in it. He hurried to be out the door before it died away.

Chapter 8
Bonefrost in Battle

When they set out in the morning they were in heavy darkness, because of the woods on either side of the road, but the narrow strip of sky they could see above was frost-grey, lit by the westering moon. It was still almost full, but it was invisible to them, hidden by the trees.

Juggler shook in his mailshirt, despite the padded undercoat he wore beneath it. A faint jingling noise around him suggested that the others in mail felt the chill, too. He had fallen asleep late and wished he could have slept late. Fighting for Garis did not seem a reasonable sort of thing to be doing, so early in the morning. But it was a little too late for him to decide that the battle was ill-advised.

The larger part of the host, and on foot, wearing leather for armor, could not be heard, but their dragging pace suggested that they felt much the same misgivings Juggler did.

Garis leaned towards Juggler. "Can you sing them faster?"

"Not unless they join in with it—and I don't think you want that much racket?"

Garis shook his head regretfully.

The strip of silver sky above them turned darker, as the moon set, and then lighter again, moving into grey towards blue. As they went by a yew tree, a puff of breeze sprang up, and thick swirls of pollen rose about them like a cloud of smoke from the dark green needles.

Across the road, another tree was loaded with the little round buds that would turn into red berries.

The sun rose, still hidden from them by the trees, but the cloud of pollen in the air above turned gold.

When the wall around the castle came into sight, they could see it, grey stone against a sky already blue. Astonished watchmen could be glimpsed peering over the ledge at them, and a bustle behind them suggested that guards had been called and were already massing behind the wall.

Eldwin rode forward and gave challenge. "Here is Garis, the son of Garis, the king of Emmering. Will you open the gates and surrender to him?"

Some of the guards laughed, but it was too early in the morning for enjoying a joke much.

The captain of the watch had already sent someone to wake the king, at their approach. He turned to the guard beside him. "Go sound an alarm—and sound a call to battle."

At Garis's side Bonefrost began to glow, a line of blue radiance in the grey dawning.

"To battle?" said the guard. "That rabble?"

"I'm a cautious man," said the captain. "Don't dawdle."

In the village on the other side of the road there was no sign of motion. It was evidently the villagers' opinion that it was the king's business to defend his own.

Garis's army split into three. One group, mostly Eldwin's people, took rams and ladders and headed for the gates, sheltered a little by a thin row of riders in mail beside them, holding shields above them. Garis waited behind this group, with Juggler beside him, and Eldwin sent off the other two groups along the walls, one to each side.

They were mostly forced workers, with the remainder of Eldwin's servants scattered among them, and they snatched up their ladders and ran for the opposite sides of the wall at a speed that showed fear of the archers gathering on the height above them, if not any enthusiasm for their cause. Already some of the army had melted away, veering off to the sides to reach the woods instead of the wall.

The archers, not knowing what this strategy might mean, shot impartially at all, and caught some.

The last of the forced workers being chivvied into the charge turned for a moment and looked venomously over his end of the ladder at Garis, before the ladder dragged him away to the stones of the wall.

Then a guard screamed and toppled over the wall, turning once in the air before hitting the ground. The arrow in his back flashed in the sunlight. His body cut a gash in the slope at the bottom of the ditch.

There were more screams, and the guards were looking in all directions. The reluctant workers setting ladders against the wall stood where they were, not setting foot on the rungs, and no one urged them on. Nester, a few rungs up one ladder, looked over at Garis, and scrambled back down again.

A few of the workers farthest from the wall broke away, trying to get to the shelter of the woods. The archers shot them down.

Still Garis waited.

The gates cracked, and bulged outward. They were opening.

"Ride!" said Garis. He galloped forward, Eldwin at his side, and Juggler, too frightened to respond quickly, a few strides behind. The horse, better trained, brought him level with the other two before they reached the gates. The first few of Eldwin's servants, closest to the gates, were the first in. Most of them fell in the entry way, speared from above through the hole over the entrance. Then a guard's body fell down through the murder hole.

Then the riders were pouring through the gateway, and workers on foot after them. The side forces abandoned their ladders entirely. A few more fled to the trees and, reaching safety there, vanished into the green shadows. But the rest, caught up by the unexpected success, came pelting to the center, jamming into a hot, smelly crowd for what seemed an endless time in which they should all have been smothered.

Then they were through the gateway, able to breathe, and spreading out on the palace grounds.

Dale was visible for a moment, resplendent in green and gold, heading a stand on the steps into the castle. But more of Garis's troop from the dungeons came bursting from the castle door, and Dale leaped to the side and was lost from sight before they could surround him.

Within the grounds the horses were no longer an advantage. There was not much room to give force to a stroke by riding into it, and there were too many obstacles to the movement of such large creatures. The guards were using benches, trees, even tubbed and potted plants as cover.

Garis dismounted, sliding off his horse with a shout of excitement. He ran headlong into the fight, unable to feel the weakness of his foot in the fever of hitting out at last. Bonefrost blazed in his hand, too bright to look at.

Juggler got down reluctantly, not certain where to strike, or how.

The folk pouring in behind him forced his direction for him.

He was pressed forward in the mass, at first unable to reach anyone in the fine armor and robes of Dale's courtiers.

The first enemy combatant he reached stopped him cold. It was Bramble, unconscious on the ground, blood running down the side of her face, and one stilt, scarred where she had struck someone with it, beside her.

Juggler raged silently, not sure if his anger was at Garis, Dale, or Bramble. He stood his ground, straddling the child's body, and elbowing his cohorts aside. At some point a guardsman took a swing at him, correctly identifying him as an opponent. Juggler swung back wildly with his axe. He escaped injury, more because of the jostling of the other struggles around them than because of skill. In a few moments more he was alone. The press of the battle had moved away, taking his assailant with it. Juggler knelt and touched Bramble's wrist. The little idiot was alive.

He gathered her up and deposited her under a rose bush in one of the higher tubs of earth, wrapping the girl's cloak about her head as pillow and bandage. There was no time to do more. Someone else was coming at him with a sword and waving energetically. He ran to catch up with the center of the battle, where he was less distinct as a target.

After a time, although he could not tell if it was short or long, or how he had come so near the castle wall, he found himself getting close to Garis, who was slowly pursuing Dale. The king, marked out by the glitter of the gold embroidery of his robe, was protected by a ring of guards. He was trying to lead them to retreat to the castle wall, to have some shelter at their backs. Somehow, someone among the guards had recognized or guessed Garis's sword. A voice cried, "Bonefrost! The manslayer!" and for a moment the castle's defenders were drawing away to the sides, but Dale called out firmly, "You fools, we want the wall!" and the guard-captain, calling even louder, repeated, "The wall!" and they drew in again, retreating in good order. Fear was one thing, but they were professionals, trained in obedience, and habit was stronger than fear. On Garis's side, though, the guards' moment of edging away gave the attackers fresh heart. They pressed in closer on the retreat. Juggler and some of the others with him set about trying to work around behind the guards to get between them and the wall to help spoil Dale's strategy.

Juggler's change of heading, toward the wall, caught Dale's attention. The king jumped to the edge of his ring of protectors and leaned out, swinging his sword against Juggler's chest. The angle of the blow was awkward, and it did not cut through his mail. All it did was to slam him back against the others with him. Dale did not spare him further attention, but struck at the next in line.

In the same moment Garis broke through the ring.

Someone short, in mail too large, darted forward and thrust a shield between Garis and the king.

It was Dianor. For a moment she and Garis stared at each other, forgetting the uproar around them. Then Garis tried to shove past her. She swung at him, and he stepped away from the blow. She could not turn the stroke to reach him, so she kept going, and landed her sword on the nearest of the attackers, hitting Juggler solidly on the elbow.

He was surprised at the clarity of his thought and ability to observe. The blow, inflicting no wound on him, thanks to his mailshirt, was still completely disabling. The axe fell from his hand. His whole side felt as if it was on fire. He tried to take a step, stumbled with it, and collapsed.

But the ring was broken. Someone else with an axe jumped in. The axe struck, and Bonefrost struck, and shields got in the way of both blows, but more followed. The green and gold went down, and Dale did not get up.

The guards scattered, and Dianor was drawn away with them.

Juggler tried to climb to his feet to follow them, but he still could not use his arm, and someone tripped over him, and someone kicked him trying to avoid a fall, and he could not find his feet or catch his breath.

There was another knot of guards farther off. Like Dianor, Lyndred had managed to get into armor before entering the fight. He carried no shield, and Juggler could not see his face, but he recognized his voice as Lyndred shouted "To me!" with a purity of tone and power that cut across the field and would have thrilled the ear if it had been in song. His voice marked him as surely as if he had flown a banner of blue and silver.

The guards answered, and so did the attackers. Someone who had snatched up Bramble's stilt was bearing down on them. It looked like Nester, improbable as that seemed.

Garis could not get through the mass of bodies to challenge Lyndred. Juggler, still held by the odd clearness of his vision, watched Garis push through the crowd, trying to force his way through to Lyndred. But the crowd itself was trying to shove forward at the same time.

Feet kept trampling over Juggler, and the clarity of vision ended in a wave of darkness.

When he woke, and his eyes cleared, he could not see Lyndred anymore. The guards seemed to have succeeded in gathering together at the wall to make a stand, but the stand did not seem to have any heart to it. They were trapped.

The archers from among Garis's dungeon troops were nosing about the ground for spent arrows, and finding them. The archers among Dale's guards held too small a space to search far enough to recover many arrows.

Someone among Garis's archers had already found and shot at least one arrow successfully. The captain of the guards had one sticking out of his shoulder. Another guard was holding him in his arms. Dreamily, Juggler recognized the support as Mulben, the captain's pet aversion.

The captain was saying something, and Mulben leaned close to him, but shook his head, as unable to make out the words. Mulben gently set the captain down on red grass and took his sword from him. Arms down at his side, a sword in each hand trailing point down and back, he turned to the forces about him, and gaped, seeing who led them. "You—" he said, stopped short, but then went on again in a rush, as someone beside Garis bent a bow. "I yield me," Mulben shouted. "I yield me," he repeated, not quite so loud, "if you'll give me my life." He rubbed his nose, sneezed, and stood sniffling.

"Yes," Garis answered, and put a hand on the archer's shoulder.

The archer waited, bow still bent, but not moving.

Garis looked around at the other guards and the courtiers among them.

Mulben put both swords on the ground at his feet and folded his arms across his chest. One by one, at first, and then all in a mass together, the rest followed him.

Dianor was among the last.

Garis beckoned to two of Eldwin's servants and nodded to them to go to Dianor.

Her gaze was fixed on him, rigid with anger and astonishment.

Garis met her glance for a moment, but then looked away. "Take Lady Dianor off the field and see her lodged somewhere befitting her rank. She'll want news of her kinsmen. Bring her word as soon as you know." He looked about, but he could not see either Dale or his son. They were not among those still standing. "Tell her—" He gave it up and waved them away.

Juggler picked himself off the ground with less difficulty than he would have expected and went to Garis. The light of Bonefrost was fading, and Garis had shifted his weight to stand entirely on his good foot. Juggler edged up against him, as if out of curiosity to see what was happening.

Garis looked back sharply.

"Only me," said Juggler, steadying him.

Garis said nothing, watching as Eldwin's servants came up to Dianor, but he leaned back, relaxing a little against Juggler's unobtrusive support.

The two servants bowed to Dianor. She looked as if she would have preferred to spit in their faces, but pride held her back, and she marched from the field, keeping a pace in front of her escort and holding her head high.

Lady Eldwin walked slowly over to them. She was limping, but it seemed to be from weariness or rheumatism, not from any wound. "You still mean to set them free, your majesty?" she said, pointing at the guards.

It took Garis a moment to realize that he was being addressed. "With conditions, yes," he said.

She frowned. "If they join with any of the troops who are out patrolling—"

"Then we'll stand a siege," Garis interrupted, finishing the sentence for her.

"As may well be." She clicked her tongue. "I think I'd better start this straightaway and proclaim you through the kingdom —to your likely supporters first, of course."

"You need rest," said Garis.

"I'll take it later." She counted off allegiances to herself on her fingers. "I don't think Norcote's friends can raise a battle against you. He ruled too heavily, and they don't like him—not enough. All the same, you'll be safer with friends declared. Have I your leave?"

Garis nodded.

She embraced him, and limped away to call her horse.

Behind her came Breredon the steward, hitching up his mail to get at the pockets of his tunic. He held up his tablets and a stick of chalk for Garis to observe, and without waiting for further orders set about recording those present on both sides —the dead, the wounded, and those unhurt, with their names, when he knew or could learn them.

Dikon, lying on the ground with a cut down his side, waved a large hand at Garis and whistled to the thin, fair woman who had been his assistant in the dungeon meetings. She clicked her tongue impatiently at finding herself needed and the need not one she'd already taken into account. She came dashing over to Garis to ask his orders.

"Send someone for the healer," he started.

"—oh, I already, sir," she interrupted.

Dikon tried to make a face at her, but found that the effort was pulling on his wounded side, and gave it up.

She had already caught the look, and seen its meaning. She made another tsking noise, and corrected herself: "—your majesty, that is."

Garis chuckled, amused in spite of himself at her mixture of confusion and efficiency. "Thanks, Flicker. And get some teams together to find planks and start getting the wounded indoors—here, and there are some outside the walls, too." He looked around and spotted Nester, exhausted, but unhurt. Garis nodded, pointing him out to Flicker. "He knows the ones outside —ask him to help. Then Dale's people—the guards'll have to go in rooms we can lock, but try to find places with some light and air to them. And send someone to cry through the castle that it's safe to come out. I have things to say, if they want to come out and hear."

"But shouldn't you—" she said.

"You should—" Juggler began at the same moment.

"No, I shouldn't look to myself until this mess is cleared up," said Garis, cutting in on them both. "But have someone bring out a stool for me. Off you go."

"Yes, your majesty."

Flicker's work soon produced a whirl of activity. Garis's stool was the first result, either because the task was the simplest or because she had revised the order of her directions. He sat down with a sigh.

Juggler started to leave him to go see that Bramble was taken care of, but decided regretfully that he should wait where he was to be useful in case any of the soldiers chose not to feel bound by Mulben's surrender. He managed to catch Flicker's eye and jerked his thumb in the direction of the rose tubs. She looked, raised her eyebrows in surprise at the occupant, and gave him a nod.

There seemed to be plenty of people showing up with bandages and boards. Flicker interfered to the extent of sending one immediately to Dikon and another to see to Bramble, then was off among them, taking charge of problems as they came to her. Under her direction, wounds were bound up and the wounded borne away, and they all seemed to be making a quick job of it.

More slowly, the palace servants and courtiers who had not taken part in the fight arrived and were directed politely enough to stand by Dale's soldiers.

When it seemed that most of those who would come out had done so, Garis drew Bonefrost and laid it across his knees. A dim light shone along the blade, glittering if he moved his legs at all. The edge had only a little of its sharpness left after hard fighting. It would have to be honed again.

Garis announced himself to them as Garis, the son of Garis the king.

"Think shame to yourself!" said the cook. "You're Garis the cleaning-boy."

"That, too," he agreed. He smiled at her. "A king could do worse than learn how to sweep a room clean."

She looked around at the stained and trampled grass, and snorted. "That's what you call it?"

"Not yet, but I'll try." He looked at the guards. "You fighters — you won't want to serve me, and if you did we couldn't trust each other. I banish you and your fellows from Emmering for two rounds of the seasons—go past the patrols in your way and give them word. Go in peace, and when you return, I promise to find you work."

"Our own work?" said Mulben.

"Not with me. With the nobles and some of the guilds—maybe. More likely other kinds of work. Less interesting, I suppose, and I'm sorry."

"Field work," said one of the soldier bitterly, although he was trying to control his voice.

"Your families might like that," said Garis. "I don't insist on it. Less danger, if that's any comfort to you."

"Less pay."

"That's like enough," said Garis. He counted to himself a moment. "At last year's prices, it's certain." He looked at the soldier thoughtfully, and at Mulben, and the rest, and their captain, on the ground in front of them. One of Flicker's assistants was kneeling by the captain, tending to him.

The soldiers, their own attention caught by seeing where Garis was looking, shifted uneasily, taking note that the wounded on their own side were being helped, but not sure what to make of it.

"Will you take to trading?" Garis asked. "If there's grain to sell in Melibos, and King Wyrond starts letting more of it come across the river, prices will improve, I think. I mean to prod the guild to open the ways and lower the duties. They should be able to make up the loss in more goods and not so much need to fight the smugglers' competition."

Again there was a stir among the soldiers. Trade sounded promising to some of them.

A courtier said, "You can't do any of that without help from King Wyrond."

"Will you go to Melibos and argue it for me?" Garis asked him quickly.

The courtier looked taken aback. "I don't know."

"Think about it." Garis looked at the rest of the courtiers and at the servants. "If you will serve me, I will dare to trust you. Stay or go, and I will help you as I may." He turned back to the guards. "My lady Eldwin is raising the lords now on my behalf. I'll let you out in three days—by then some of your fellows who were hurt will be able to travel with you, with your help. If you think she'll fail to find me support, of course, you'll want to set a siege—if you can."

Mulben did not look particularly eager to take up the choice. Others looked more interested, but not as sure of the odds as they would have liked to be.

Garis turned to the cook. "Don't decide about putting up with me yet—but will you feed us for the next few days?"

"I'd need—"

"Tell Flicker." Garis looked around for her and beckoned. "Lock them up—except anyone the cook wants—and let's start getting people fed. If that list of who's here is finished, you and Breredon can get people assigned to beds."

She looked at him quizzically.

He turned pink and coughed. "Whatever choices you think best, Flicker."

There was a confusion of noises, and groups shifting this way and that, and mostly getting in each other's way, and for some moments it seemed that no one would get anywhere. Then suddenly there were ways clear and people following them, and in a few moments more the crowd had disappeared within-doors, some guarding and some guarded, some walking and some carried.

Garis looked about for his crutch, but it was nowhere in sight. He had left it in the spear-rest when he had dismounted, but it could hardly have stayed in place there without a rider.

The horses, sensibly, had fled from the commotion as far as they could go, and were clustered against the wall.

One of Flicker's team was already setting off to begin soothing them and gathering them in to shelter.

Another of them found Garis's crutch and brought it to him.

When the prisoners were gone, Juggler helped him stand up, and Garis entered into his castle.

Chapter 9
The Two Kings

Breredon found them as they came through the hall. "With your approval, sire, we have put you both into Lord Lyndred's room." The steward was evidently acting in cooperation with Flicker.

Garis exchanged a glance with Juggler. "Where's Lyndred?" he asked.

"Dead," said Breredon quietly.

Garis nodded. "What about Dale?"

"He is alive, but badly hurt. I have put him in his own room, under guard."

"How do the numbers stand?"

"Better than we expected," Breredon said. "Many died outside the walls, but not so many ran away as I had guessed. Inside, a good many injured, but only a few killed." He took a leaf from his tablets and handed it to Garis. "I'll have a better record ready for you later," he said. "I need to locate an ink-horn." He bowed and hurried on with his work.

Garis started to look at the listing, but tears came into his eyes, and he could not read. He crumpled it up, then thought better of that, smoothed it out, and rolled it up, and went to Lyndred's room to rest until some food was ready.

The list would keep.

A pallet had been put into the room, set next to Lyndred's bed. Juggler thought about the distance down it would be to get from standing to lying. His bruises had stiffened, and to stand seemed easier than to reach the pallet. Instead, he helped Garis lie down on the bed and then went to look for the rooms where the injured had been put. There would be willowbark tea there. He could take a cup for himself and another to force down Garis, and perhaps he could find out how Bramble was.

The youngster was awake. There had not been time yet for the healer to get round to less serious injuries, but several of the guards had some training in the elements of physic. Bramble's head was neatly bandaged. She was sitting up in a bed, with her arms hugging her knees, apparently unaware of the bustle around her. Most of those who had been hurt had been put into one of the sleeping rooms for the servants, and there was not really enough room for them. More pallets and a ragged assortment of coverings were being brought in. Spaces to set them all were getting hard to come by.

Juggler squeezed through and had to wave before he got Bramble's attention. He sat down, carefully, on the edge of the bed. "How do you feel?"

"Is it true, what they're saying?" Bramble said, by way of answer.

"Depends what they're saying."

"Everyone who fought for the king is banished."

After a moment's thought, Juggler said, "That doesn't mean you."

"How do you know?"

"Garis wouldn't do that."

"Garis?" Bramble was obviously disbelieving. Then, seeing that Juggler was serious, she looked more hopeful, for a moment. Then another reflection cast her into gloom. "My mother wanted to see me, and they wouldn't let her in. She said to tell me if I'm banished I could go stay with her cousins twice removed in the weaver's guild, and I don't know them, and I don't know any weaving, and I don't want to."

Bramble's parents worried over what to do with a daughter who did not take to cooking. They might be thinking it was time to find an apprenticeship for the girl, regardless of what Garis might say about banishment. But perhaps they would listen if Juggler suggested that there was time for that later, when the youngster was not quite so young. Or, better still, perhaps they would listen if Garis suggested it. "I don't think you'll have to go anywhere," he told her.

"You're not sure," said Bramble accusingly.

"No, but I don't think so."

Bramble shook her head.

Juggler sat for a while, considering the girl's alternatives. At length he said, "Bramble, your trouble is that you're scared, your head hurts, and you have nothing to do but sit around going over your troubles."

"I'm not scared!"

"How about worried?"

"Maybe."

"I can't help with most of that, but if you feel up to it tomorrow, I can give you something to do."

"What?" Bramble said suspiciously.

"Copying some old books. If you can find out who else here can write and would be glad of a little occupation, that would be a help, too."

This time he had her attention. The project was absurd enough to win a reluctant smile from the girl. "I guess so," she said. "But why?"

"The sorcerer Hluvend wants books. He helped us, and that's what he asked by way of payment."

"You saw a sorcerer? A real one? Did he work magic?"

"I think he's real, and I think he worked real magic. Come to think of it, I'm not sure. We spent more time helping delousing his chickens."

"You didn't!"

"Even sorcerer's chickens need looking after."

Bramble looked contemptuous. "Then he ought to have a magic spell against lice."

"Either he didn't, or it's less work to go at it the usual way," said Juggler.

Bramble found this idea too confusing to work out, but it seemed to have improved matters slightly. The muscles in her shoulders suddenly relaxed, and she blinked several times. Then she yawned twice.

"Try lying down," said Juggler.

"I guess so." Bramble lowered her head carefully to the pillow, and stretched her legs out straight. After a few moments she was asleep.

Juggler looked around the room, missing the herb tea at first, because the urn was covered with a cloth to keep warm a little longer than it would otherwise. A pile of cups on the floor beside it gave away the location, and Juggler went there. Moving carefully, he bent down and hunted among the cups until he found two that had not been used, then poured himself a cup. Despite the cloth, it was almost cold. He wrinkled his nose at the bitter smell, and gulped it down. Then he swallowed several times, trying to get the taste out of his mouth, and poured another cup to take to Garis.

Corbian, the healer, was a tall woman, and stout besides. Even tired out, her presence filled the room. She stared down, first at Juggler, then at Garis. "So you think you're king," she said.

"A beginning of one."

"I don't like your beginning."

Garis made no reply.

"Well, let's see." Corbian leaned over and untied the dirty bandage on his foot. She poked the foot, turned it this way and that to see which directions hurt him and how much, and then rebound it with clean bandage. "You know well enough what to do for that," she said. "Stay off it." She looked at the crutch on the floor beside the bed. "That's well enough," she said, "but you'll balance better and feel less uncomfortable on a pair." She pulled out a ball of string and measured it against his length, from armpit to foot, then knotted it. "I'll see about getting them for you."

"Thank you," said Garis.

She nodded, a gesture that apparently was meant to cover making a bow, and turned as if about to go.

"How long will I need them?"

"As long as it hurts," she said impatiently.

"How long is that?"

She relented, turning back. "Hard to say. A week, certainly. Probably a few weeks. Even a few months, but more than two would surprise me."

"And then it'll be well?"

"I don't know that, either." Corbian pursed her lips. "I *think,* young man, and mind I say, I think, that you will always limp. You cannot run about on pure spirit as much as you have been doing and expect your body to heal it all up after you."

"I see. Thank you, Corbian." Garis lay back on his pillow. "You'll come by tomorrow to see how the injured are doing?"

"Cats chase birds," she answered. "I suppose I am to check the guards as well as your own people?"

Garis managed a weak laugh. "Don't set traps for me. They're both my people."

"Are they so?" She nodded briskly. "And they're all my patients—as are you. I will watch the progress accordingly." She gathered up the old bandages to be cleaned, and strode from the room without any further leave-taking.

Supper was not as jubilant a meal as they had expected for what was, after all, a victory feast, or meant to be. Most of them were in some pain, even if it was only bruises, and the knowledge that taking the castle was, after all, not the same thing as taking the kingdom was disquieting. Also, the food was not very good.

Breredon scrupulously explained that this was his fault, not the cook's—who appeared to him to be doing her best. But the battle had disrupted the morning's normal purchases, and he did not know where to buy what supplies for what prices as well as the castle's own steward did.

Juggler could not think of any subject for conversation except Bramble, and as that topic did not seem to him a cheerful one, he was silent at first. But the subject of injuries came up, and rather than listen to everyone at the table detailing his or hers, Juggler brought up the youngster after all, and repeated the conversation they had held.

Garis sighed. "Thanks for reassuring her," he said. "She's welcome to stay if I can talk her parents into letting her—I'll have to talk to everyone, eventually, I suppose. But there'll be some who'll want to go, no matter what I might offer—not to mention some I'll want to see gone no matter what they might offer."

"Going to help all of them find new places, are you?" said Dikon skeptically. He was not, perhaps, quite well enough to be sitting up, but he had come anyway.

"If you'll count 'trying to help' the same as 'helping'—yes. If you mean how many will find work close to what they've had here—I won't really have much idea until I see which of the nobles show up in my favor."

This led them to a discussion of which nobles to expect and what decisions they might expect of the various courtiers and servants. The courtiers, they thought, would mostly go, and the servants mostly stay.

Breredon was of the opinion that the castle steward would go, for he was old, and had been with Dale when Dale was only lord of Norcote. "It's too bad," said Breredon. "You won't find anyone that sound on both the value of money and the value of good food." He waved apologetically at their own board by way of demonstration. "He's a little weak in fabrics, though," he added thoughtfully. "You want someone who knows which stuff will wash, for instance, and how much is too much for a good velvet."

"One of his assistants, maybe," said Garis.

Breredon did not dispute this as a possibility, but he looked doubtful.

"You'd do better with one of our thieves," said Flicker. "They know the value of everything."

Garis chuckled. "That's a thought."

They left the table feeling more cheerful than had seemed likely when they sat down to it.

In the morning Garis nerved himself to go through Lyndred's clothes, looking for something he could wear. The things fit well enough, except for being a trifle long, but most of them were of blue and silver, which Garis would not wear, or of green and gold, which he did not want to wear yet. At last he found a plain green linen tunic, the color faded to greyish-green. He suspected that Breredon, even if he didn't say it, would think that a prince's clothes should be dyed in colors that lasted better than that, but it was the best he could do for the time being. He added a swordbelt in order to keep Bonefrost with him, and a gold circlet on his head.

Corbian had sent a pair of crutches, as promised, and a black felt slipper large enough to go on his foot over the bandages. He could not find anything to match it. With a shrug, he took a brown leather slipper for the other foot.

He stood up, and took a few steps. Corbian was right— walking was easier with support on both sides. But moving quickly was more difficult. "Come with me, will you?" he said to Juggler. He did not want to be obviously guarded, but he didn't want to limp around the halls alone, either.

They went to Dale's room. A man was guarding the door. He bowed to Garis, and opened the door for him.

Dale was in bed, attended by Dianor and her nurse Rosewind. Dale's face was ashy, and although he said something at sight of Garis, it was lost in the clatter as Dianor jumped up, knocking over her stool.

Bonefrost shone with a bright blue light.

"My lady—" said Garis.

Juggler tried to get in the way, but she moved too fast for him, reaching Garis in two long strides, her hands clenching into a pair of fists.

She struck Garis just under the chin with the full force of her own strength and the speed she was going.

Garis reeled back, dropping his crutches to the floor. Juggler leaned sideways and caught him around the waist, so that Garis fell against him instead of falling all the way down. The force shoved them both up against the wall, catching some of Juggler's bruises painfully.

Juggler gasped, then caught his breath and his balance, propped Garis against the wall, and looked around to see what more was happening.

Dale was trying to sit up in bed.

Garis's guard had rushed in to try to seize the princess, but her nurse had forestalled him and had Dianor caught, one arm twisted behind her.

Dale settled back in bed and looked them over. "Water," he said.

His voice was too feeble to be heard over the uproar, but the shape of the word on his lips was distinct.

Juggler found the pitcher, poured a cup, and started to offer it to Dale.

Dale raised an eyebrow at this stupidity, and pointed a finger at Garis.

Juggler about-faced and went back. He helped Garis sip the water, while the guard picked up the crutches and set them under Garis's arms.

"You ice-hearted nobody's son, get out of here," said Dianor, struggling unsuccessfully against Rosewind's hold.

"Child, keep that up, and you'll catch your death of cold iron, or hemp," said the nurse. She let go of Dianor's arm and spun her around to look into her face.

Dianor said nothing.

"You may not care," Rosewind told her, "but I do, and so does the king."

Dianor said nothing to that, either, but the nurse, after eyeing her a moment more, turned her attention to Garis, waiting to hear what he had to say for himself.

Garis cleared his throat, took another sip of water, and found that there was still a voice inside. "I've come to see how you are, my lord," he said to Dale.

"You don't speak to the king that way," said Dianor.

Dale smiled sardonically. He shifted a little on his pillows, trying to ease himself. "But he says he is King Garis of Emmering, as I hear—and he holds the castle," he pointed out to her.

"How are you?" Garis repeated.

"Ill enough," Dale answered readily. "I may perhaps not trouble you long."

"Perhaps you may, if you'll just put your mind to it," said Rosewind.

"A possibility," he agreed, although he did not sound as if he thought it a likely one. "And what would you do with me, in that case?" he asked Garis.

"Ask Lady Eldwin to hold you prisoner for me."

Dianor made a noise of protest. She stopped and clamped her mouth shut on it, then turned and stared coldly out the window at the clouds.

"I should not complain," said Dale. "It's what I meant for you." He paused, and tried again to shift himself. "—and better than I meant for you after I thought about it."

Garis was not surprised at the addition, but Dianor was. She stopped looking out the window and turned to look at her uncle instead.

Dale met her gaze for a moment, then turned with some difficulty again to Garis.

"You're tiring yourself," said Garis. "I'd better go."

"Do you really think you can afford to keep me?" said Dale. "I'll be the focus for every malcontent with a few followers anywhere in Emmering."

"I'll worry about that if I have to," said Garis, "but not until then." He started toward the door.

"Wait!" said Dale.

"Yes?"

"People are keeping things from me. For my own good, I do not doubt. But you, young man, will tell me what happened to Lyndred."

"He died in the battle," said Garis, gently.

"I see." Dale was silent a moment, considering, then said, "Did you kill him?"

"Yes, I think so," Garis said reluctantly.

"You don't know?" Dianor said, disbelief in her voice.

"It has to have been a serious injury, but he was still fighting when the jostling around us pulled us apart. When Breredon gets his tallies completed, he will probably know for sure, and you can ask him. If you're sure you want to know, that is."

"Not particularly. Thank you." Dale drew the blanket up over his head so that he could not be seen weeping.

Garis turned and put out a hand, but he was not near enough to touch Dale.

"Get out!" said Dianor.

Garis thought about it, gave a sigh, and nodded. He settled his weight on the crutches and went with Juggler from the room.

In the hallway, Garis stood still a little while.

"You could go back to bed," said Juggler.

"It's a thought," said Garis, but having thought it over, he said, "Where's Breredon likely to be?—kitchen? No, storerooms, more likely."

They found Breredon with a tally-board in the pantry, and Juggler left them there to a soothing discussion of meat, fish, beer, and dried fruits and vegetables, with occasional excursions into hot water (cooking), and hot water (baths).

Juggler used the time to hunt up the manuscripts for Hluvend.

* * *

After lunch Garis set about talking to those who had not fought, with Juggler in attendance. Between them, they knew almost all the servants, and a good many of the courtiers as well. Garis had knowledge to offer among the servants. He knew what they liked of their work—such as the steward's general care in assigning it fairly, the money they earned by it, the good materials given them to work with—and he knew what they wanted besides—more places to sit down, more time for amusements of their own within a day, some time to visit friends and families. He could promise them more seats and time. Time within a day was something he was sure he could manage. It would not be much help to those whose families lived at any distance, but he thought it might be possible to do something for them, as well, assuming cooperation and a good head for details in the steward. Probably the steward, whoever it was, would need extra help to cope with the extra work involved, and they all knew that Garis was probably going to be short in skilled stewardship, at first. He promised to pay attention to the tasks of finding and training good stewards as quickly as might be.

Most of the servants were inclined to believe in the good faith of his promises. Some asked to have others dismissed as quarrelers or shirkers. The stable-hands, set as they were in a building some little distance from the others, were widely accused of laziness. Garis privately agreed with the accusation, but he did not say so. He had no intention of adding immediately to the number of his enemies if he could help it, and he firmly refused to take on the job of being firm in such matters. Dismissals were in the steward's domain.

Of the courtiers, the greater part was made up of Dale's officers of state—or would-be officers, hoping for appointment —and their families. Their offices would be going to Garis's followers, and the former place-holders and place-hunters would mostly leave, too. Some of the courtiers, however, were hostages for the good behavior of their families. Most of these hailed Garis, cautiously, as a deliverer.

There were also a good many young folk, sent to court for fostering. Dale stood to them as guardian, and relief that Garis was not planning to make hostages of them made them more cordial to him than their parents might have approved. All of them would go to their homes—and, no doubt, some of them would be sent back again. There was prestige in court fosterage, no matter who was on the throne to do the fostering.

Toward the end of the following day, Garis went with Juggler to visit the injured guardsmen.

Bramble looked up as they came in, without actually seeing them. Her absorption this time, however, was not in terror. She had a writing board on her lap, and she was deep in the poem of "The Siege of the City of the Stars," which she had kept for herself in the distribution of manuscripts to copy. It was full of maps of the stars, and she was mapping away in her copy with careful devotion to exact measurement. It was slow work, and thoroughly enjoyable for a youngster whose curiosity extended to the night skies.

By the time they reached her bed, she had noticed who they were, but her head was too full of stars to be frightened by the changes going on around her. She waved vaguely, and went on filling in the stars of the Hunter's bow.

"That's fine work," said Garis.

"Um," said Bramble in agreement. She added regretfully, "But I can't do the pictures." She turned back to a page where the Rivers beat on the doors of the City for admittance into the streets of Night.

The artist who had done the painting had contrived to suggest the terrible radiance within the City by careful use of gilding, leaking out at the hinges and over the top of the walls. The grass in the meadow was dark blue.

"Know anyone who can?" said Juggler.

Bramble shook her head, still looking at the City, but after a moment the question finished making its way into her consideration. "Lady Dianor." Speaking the name aloud drew her attention to what she was saying, and she set down the chart and gave the matter a few seconds' more thought, without coming up with anyone else with the skills for the work. "Lady Dianor," she repeated, and took up the chart again, to measure the distance between two more stars.

"Oh," said Garis.

"You could ask," said Juggler.

"Bramble, would you ask her to do it?" said Garis.

The girl shot him a puzzled glance. "Why?"

"Because you took on the job of having charge over the copying," said Garis, not quite truthfully. "If it gets to be too much for you and starts your head aching, send me word."

"I can do that."

"How *does* your head feel?" Garis added.

Bramble started to rub it, then remembered not to and took her hand away. "Not very good. But better."

"That'll do for now," said Garis.

The day after, when they went to see how Dale was, they found Dianor at work drawing rough sketches of each picture in the manuscript and making notes of the color of each segment. She looked up at them resentfully. "You again."

Juggler moved quietly into a corner where he could watch. He would have preferred to leave them alone to have their quarrel out, but with Dianor's nurse and Dale present that was impossible, even though Rosewind's attention was ostensibly fixed on setting in some button-holes, and Dale did not seem to be awake. Between Garis's need for help getting around and his own curiosity, Juggler chose to stay, as unobtrusively as he could manage.

"How is he?" said Garis.

"Worse."

"Corbian will be by here soon. Maybe she can think of something that could help."

Dianor nodded.

Garis tried again. "I don't suppose you want to be thanked for that copy work, but thank you anyway."

"You're welcome."

An uncomfortable silence followed. Dianor finished off a list of colors and sat drawing the lines of the leaves on a willow.

Garis watched the leaves grow.

At last Dianor said, "You left something out when you were telling us your plans."

"What do you want to know?"

"About me. If you want to lock me up, too, I want to be with my uncle."

"No!" said Garis.

It was obvious from voice and look that his objection was to imprisoning her at all.

"Can I visit him?"

"Yes, of— That is—" Garis thought about it. "I don't know," he said.

She put down her pen, stopped up the inkwell, and rubbed at the stains on her fingers. Without looking up, she said, "You do realize, don't you, that I'm a threat to you, too? If I married a noble with forces of his own, or if I set out myself to look for supporters to back me—"

"But—" Garis interrupted, and stopped short.

"But what?"

"I thought you'd marry me," he said, mumbling the words.

"That would neutralize the threat. But I won't be wed to please a faction—not Uncle's, and not yours. I'll have my own liking, or I'll have none." She added wryly, "And if you want it to be no one, you'd best lock me up with the king. If you leave me free, and I come to love someone not to your liking, you'll get no word of warning from me."

Garis's face went rigid. He was silent again, counting over the dangers she had set before him.

"Prison, then?" she said, mockingly. "I've plenty of work to do." She tapped the sketch, leaving a smudge.

Garis flushed. "You—"

Rosewind gathered up her threads and eyed them sternly. "You children hold your tongues! This is a sickroom, and not a thundercloud."

There was another silence, and Corbian arrived. She looked around at them with a moment's curiosity, but set it aside and went to her patient. Gently, she unwrapped the dressing on Dale's leg, and sponged clean the wound. It smelled bad, and it looked bad. Red streaks showed up and down his leg. Dale cried out at being handled, and the nurse and Dianor held him still for the healer.

Corbian beckoned them away from the bedside.

"Will you cut?" said the nurse.

Dianor started to speak, but closed her lips together and held herself silent.

"It's too high up, and he's too weak," said Corbian. "But it might be an easier death, if nothing else." She looked at Dianor. "I'll try, if you order it, my lady."

"Isn't there anything else to try?" said Dianor.

Corbian shook her head. "The wound is mortified, and the poison is spreading out from it through him."

Garis looked up at the word poison. "I wonder," he said, and then looked at Dale.

They were too preoccupied to heed him. Even the guard's attention and Juggler's were caught up in Corbian's low-voiced discussion of her patient's poor chances, and away from the patient himself.

Garis drew Bonefrost out of his belt, limped to the bed, and set the flat of the blade against Dale's leg.

The sword flashed, leaving streaks of light against his vision.

Dale screamed, and his body stiffened, arching upward. He opened his eyes for a moment and stared at Garis. Then he straightened again, falling back on the bed. He gave a sigh, and his eyelids closed.

Dianor rushed to him, but Corbian elbowed her aside.

"Murderer!" said Dianor.

"Hush," said Corbian. She felt Dale's wrist and forehead, and one of the red streaks. He was breathing evenly and did not gasp when she touched him.

The others, obediently, were hushed, waiting for her to speak, even Dianor.

Corbian gave a whistle and turned to stare at Garis. "Well!" she said. "They said you had some sorcery about you, but it was for winning battles, by what I heard."

"It's Bonefrost," said Garis. "It's supposed to be a protection against poison. Hluvend said so." He looked ill and dizzy. His hand shook, and he could not put the sword back in his belt.

"Would you like to try that trick on others in the same case?" said Corbian.

Dianor found it difficult to believe what Corbian seemed to be saying. "You mean he's all right?"

"He looks as if he will be," said the healer. "But I want to see that again."

"Yes. All right," said Garis, without moving.

Corbian called Juggler out of his safe retreat in the corner to help Garis away. She paused a moment to tell Dianor and the nurse to bind up the leg again in fresh bandages—" Do you have enough?" she said.

"Yes," said Dianor, but her tone was uncertain. It was difficult to keep a supply ready for Dale when so many needed to have bandages ready.

Garis reached under his tunic and untied the strip of cloth he had worn about his waist since the inn. He tossed it to the nurse. "A token," he said, with a shrug, and let Corbian hurry him away.

Chapter 10
Mended

Corbian found that Bonefrost did nothing to simple injuries, but only to the ones that had mortified, and only when Garis held it. The sword's magic drew strength from Garis. After several trials, she made him stop, alarmed by his pallor.

The worst hurt had been helped. The rest would have to wait their turn.

The first of the nobles summoned by Lady Eldwin had begun to arrive, bringing in their train supplies of food. Breredon was much relieved, as even his methodical ways had not yet restored order to what should have been the castle's daily purchases of goods from the nearby villages.

The villagers, used to dealing with Dale's steward, and worried about keeping enough to live on themselves until the first crops of the spring began to ripen, were holding back. Carters who brought in goods from farther off were still coming, as the word of the changes in the castle was slower to reach them, and they did not much care who came to the gate to deal with them. If Dale or his supporters objected later on to dealings they had had with his assailant, they would be farther away again, and some trouble to find. But stocks everywhere in the country were low in early spring, and a castle had many hungry bellies to feed. And even a castle's resources needed careful management to be sure of finding enough to feed them.

Thanks to the newcomers, and the supplies they brought with them, their supper the next day was lavish, ending with a procession of cakes and sweets in many flavors and colors. Garis was at first too tired to do more than look at his food and mush it around with his knife, but the desserts brought back his appetite. He sat long with his new supporters, encouraging them to tell him about themselves, a form of conversation that left most of them believing they had seen proof of his eloquence of speech and clearness of thought.

The cookery helped to strengthen this impression.

There was comfort for them also in counting each the number of the others.

Juggler was almost asleep when a rattling of the little panes of the window startled him. He looked around.

The room was dark. The window was silver, except where it was blotted by the outline of Garis, sitting with his nose pressed up to it to look out. A half-moon, still slightly pot-bellied, was rising.

Juggler sat up and began to shiver. He groped about and found two cloaks. He put one on and took the other to Garis. "It's cold," he said.

"There's a north wind," said Garis. The window rattled behind him.

The moon was floating up through long thin streaks of dark cloud.

"You'd be warmer if you went back to bed."

"I don't mind it."

"What's the trouble?"

"Nothing."

"I could sing you a lullaby," said Juggler.

"Try it, and I'll hit you."

Juggler huddled deeper into the cloak. The meaning of Garis's "Nothing" was obvious enough, and it was equally obvious that he wanted privacy to brood over it. It did not necessarily follow that he ought to have the privacy. Juggler waited a few moments longer and then said, "You can always think about her in the morning. You'll addle your wits if you try to think by moonlight after a hard day."

"I'm not thinking by the moon, I'm thinking by the wind," Garis said.

"Clearer, but colder," said Juggler.

Garis leaned against the window. "It's blowing a Winter wind," he said. "Decisions call for a cool head and careful thought."

"And what are you thinking?"

"She's right. I'll have to put her under ward." When Juggler did not immediately reply, Garis said, in a gritty voice, "Why don't you argue?"

"Because I'm cold and tired, and so are you, no matter what you think."

"Go to bed," Garis suggested.

Juggler looked wistfully at the shadows that marked his pallet in the shadows of the room. He tucked the corners of the cloak around him, trying to keep the chill out. "If you want to consider the needs of the state, take a need that will get you somewhere. Tell me the names of all the nobles and what they grow and where they trade."

"I don't know them all."

"Then tell me the ones you know, and you'll know which ones to study."

Garis grunted impatiently, but then he began to recite names and information. He could see that he was being coaxed. But he could also see that what Juggler was prompting him to bring to mind was information he needed to have ready. Slowly, he brought out the names and what he knew for each.

When he faltered, Juggler said, "You know more of them than that. Lie down and think a bit, and see how many you can add."

"I see through that," said Garis, but he turned away from the north wind and crawled back to his bed.

Juggler felt his way through the shadows to his pallet and dropped into it, without even taking off the cloak.

Garis started reciting again, but his voice slowed, and when he started repeating himself Juggler stopped paying attention. Even before he finished drifting back to sleep the recitation had ended.

The next day Dikon was well enough to leave his bed, and Garis called a meeting of the nobles and the leaders of his army of conspirators. It was an uneasy session. Everyone there expected, reasonably enough, to be rewarded for loyalty. There were not enough favors, appointments, or monies to go around if all were to be rewarded according to their wishes.

Garis carefully avoided making any firm grants. After all, as he pointed out, he was not yet even crowned. He needed to know better what was available.

He began by asking who lived on bad roads and could get crops to market more cheaply if the roads were better, and who could make use of trade directly across the river with Melibos.

A noble with estates along the river asked if the merchants' guild had been consulted.

"Not yet," said Garis.

The noble raised her eyebrows.

"No, first I consult my friends," said Garis. "But I've been reading the guild records," he added. "I've noticed that the merchants worry most about controlling the most expensive goods—and that means the ones from furthest away, usually. I don't think they'll object if we want to bring in goods from Melibos."

"They'll want a share," she pointed out.

"No reason they shouldn't," said Garis.

This answer proved acceptable, and his reluctance to enter into promises immediately seemed understandable to them. Eventually, after considerable discussion, one of the nobles suggested that they set the date for his coronation. The ceremony would not increase Garis's knowledge or the throne's resources, but it would give a look of more substance to any grants he made.

They settled on a week. By then many of the outlying nobles would have arrived, and the supplies the nobles already there had brought would maintain them for that long without sending to their homes for more or straining the district's resources. It would also keep large forces at the castle during the period when Dale's soldiers could most easily try to rally support for a counterattack, before Garis could reasonably set about enforcing their banishment.

Garis then tried to steer the conversation to such educational questions as who had the most luck trading which crops in what manner through which traders, but his allies were still interested in the subject of his coronation. Lord Hopworth, a big man with a wide jaw and a wide body, and as stubborn as he looked, said, "Just yourself to be crowned, sire, or will you give us a queen, too?"

"Just me," said Garis.

"If you have no objection to Lady Dianor," his ally said helpfully, "it would be wise—"

"She objects to me," Garis interrupted, and went back to crops.

Lord Hopworth looked as if he would have liked to give more good advice on the topic, but someone on one side or the other of him had more tact and nudged him. He jerked in his chair, and dropped the subject.

When Garis could get away from his supporters he went to Dale's room. Dale made no sign when he came in, and Garis looked anxiously at Dianor and Rosewind.

"He isn't very well just now," Rosewind said, answering the question implied. "He has a fever. But Corbian says he's getting better."

Garis nodded and sat down.

Dianor was cracking eggs and separating the whites. She then uncovered a bowl with a thick dark mud in it. She added some spoonfuls of the stuff to the egg-white and began stirring. The mixture turned to a clear willow green. She took a brush and tried a dab of the stuff on a piece of blank paper. It was gooey. She added a little water and stirred some more. Then she took up her line drawings and her sketches with color notes, and began filling in the green spaces.

Garis sat watching her, enjoying the silence. Outside there were things he should be doing, all calling for discussion. They could wait.

When the mix was mostly gone, Dianor added more egg-white and stirred in more of the paste of pigment. Several of the drawings by then were spread out on the floor, and the first was dry. She took up the City of the Stars and began filling in a green River's robe.

Dale stirred, and Rosewind gave him some water.

The motion seemed to be a counter-charm against the silence they had kept.

Dianor glanced at him, and said, "Have you decided what I am to do?"

"Yes," said Garis. He took a breath and let it out. "Go free, when you choose."

She held her brush over the bowl so that it would not matter if it dripped, and stared at him. "Is that good policy, do you think?"

"I don't know. I *can't* know."

She started filling in the greens again. "What do you mean?" she said, without looking at him.

Garis looked at the color growing on the page for a few moments more. "I want to lock you up to stop you from marrying anyone else," he said. "I can't tell if I think shutting you in would be good statecraft—too much jealousy in the way. And you wanted to follow the river...and I wanted you to be happy.... So ...."

Dianor waited, but he had run out of explanation. She glanced at her uncle, and sighed. She put the City down to dry and said, "You'd better go."

Dale said, "Don't say goodnight and leave, Dianor."

"He's wandering," said Dianor. She started clearing away her paint and papers to go to him.

"I am not wandering," said Dale. He opened his eyes and blinked at the daylight in the room. "—except perhaps as to the time of day. I know very well who you are. You are Dianor, and you mean to love someone else. But you don't. The more fool you to think you can." He closed his eyes.

Dianor found a path through the litter around her. She dampened a cloth and laid it on Dale's forehead. "He thinks I'm someone else," she said.

"That's as may be," said Rosewind, "but he's right for all of that. She does love you, young man."

"I don't—"

"I have eyes in my head, I hope," the nurse retorted. She used them to glance from Dianor to Garis and back again. "Furthermore, he loves you. I don't know if you'd noticed."

"He doesn't—"

"I love you, Dianor." Garis thought it was time for him to take a hand in his wooing, no matter how hopeless it was likely to be, rather than leave it all to be done for him by his enemies.

She looked around at them all, doubtfully.

Garis said glumly, "The river alone, or someone else, or me. Choose your liking." He tried to stand up to look at her directly.

Dianor reached out and helped him up.

He wanted to keep hold of her hands, but he forced himself to let go. "My lady?" he said.

Dianor tried to speak, but could not find words. She took his hands again.

He bent his head and kissed her.

They stood there for a long time. Or it could have been no time. They were not sure which.

The watchman at the door knocked and said, "Beg pardon, sir. Dikon says there's representatives come from the guilds to see you."

It was a double coronation after all. Lord Hopworth took credit to himself for arranging it.

Dale, once he was properly awake and understood that he had more or less approved the match, approved it again. He said it was a wise step for Dianor to take—a remark that almost made her want to break it off again. He declined to give them a blessing, however, either formally at the coronation or in private. "You can't afford to have me seen in public," he told Garis. "And while it might perhaps be in my best interests to be helpful to you in secret, I do not think that is the case. You could only free me if you trusted my word, and that, of course, you cannot do."

"But if you gave your word—" Dianor began.

"I gave it to his father, and broke that. I am well served for it. The boy's a fool, Dianor, and maybe you could talk him round. But he killed Lyndred, and even if I thought it could do me any good to offer my word, I will not offer it to him." Dale closed his eyes a moment, took a breath, and let it out again. "I'm tired," he said gently. "Go away."

After that Garis did not try to visit him.

There was plenty of work for Garis to do elsewhere. He found time among other chores to order the gilding stripped from the throne and put into the treasury. He went after the scarlet himself, first with water and ground deerhorn, then with spirits of wood vinegar and spirits of pine oil. With these he thinned the layers of paint enough for the carved roots and blossoms to show their lines clearly. In some lights, the grain of the wood shone through the remaining red.

Juggler stood as Dianor's father, and Eldwin returned in time for the coronation and stood as Garis's mother.

Their substitute parents brought them from the throne into the ritual-hall at noon of the day appointed. A table was ready in the center. The season being so early, there was no wheat for them to plait, but there was straw, and Bramble served them bowls of hot water with flour mixed in to make a paste.

They stood at the table and worked carefully, Garis leaning now on a cane only, instead of a pair of crutches, and Dianor at his side, breaking the straw into even lengths, and pasting the individual straws together to make segments of a reasonable thickness. They pressed the sections together, end to end, setting the joins with more paste, until they had completed a circle each.

These were the crowns of ceremony, made by groom and king, bride and queen alike. For lesser occasions, king and queen would wear gold, but at the times of high ceremony, those who undertook to wear crowns were expected to build them anew.

The straw gave off a warm smell that gradually filled the room.

While Dianor and Garis washed the paste off their hands, Eldwin and Juggler made the circuit of the room, showing the crowns to the statues of the gods, and then gave them back. Dianor and Garis crowned each other as husband and wife. Then they made the circle of the gods themselves, and re-assumed the crowns, this time crowning themselves.

The witnesses shouted, hailing the king and queen.

They should have danced then, but Garis could not, and Dianor said, looking at the keyboard of the pipe-organ, "I'd just as soon not hear it."

"The others will want to dance, though," said Garis.

"There's the lute," said Juggler.

"There is?" Garis was surprised. "But when did you—"

"Before we left." Juggler ran from the hall and returned with his lute. The curves of the wood caught the light, shining gold against the darkness of the grain.

Juggler put the strap over his shoulder and began tuning the strings, grunting a little at each peg, for his elbow was still stiff, but then Bramble came to his aid and turned them for him until he was satisfied with the concord of the strings.

He played, then, and his hearers listened or danced, setting aside for the moment all questions of policy. The year would bring other days to deal with them. Juggler played the sun out of the sky.

The manuscripts for Hluvend were ready, in a satchel, which Juggler had left under the keyboard.

The dancers had given up, pair by pair, and gone in search of the table set with food in the Great Hall, or to find corners of privacy. The listeners, too, had gradually drifted away, into the feasting hall.

Bramble's parents had outdone themselves in the dishes. The head cook still looked doubtful over Garis, but she was, she said, curious to see what he would make of himself, and she and her husband had decided to keep Bramble with them.

Juggler paused for a little, and wriggled his fingers to ease them.

Dianor and Garis were looking at each other and no longer hearing any music outside themselves.

Juggler waved to draw their attention, and then flicked his fingers at them, shooing them away.

They blinked, turning their attention out beyond themselves, then laughed. Dianor helped Garis up, and they left the room together.

Juggler picked up the satchel of manuscripts. It seemed as good a time as any to begin. He made his way from the ritual-hall to the feast, and stuffed into the top of the bag some food he would eat within the day. Playing again, for his own pleasure, and the few guards watching at door and gate, he wandered out of the castle, and the castle grounds.

The sun was down, and the stars were out. The wind was from the south, blowing warm air around him. He shrugged his cloak back and walked over the new grass toward the rising stars.

The End

About the Author

Ruth Berman's books include a novel, *Bradamant's Quest* (FTL Publications), and a share in a group novel, *Autumn World* (FTL Publications); two chapbooks of sf/fantasy poems, *Beyond the Moones Sphere* and *To Faery Lond They Came* (self-published); *Sherlock Holmes in Oz and others* (Norwegian Explorers of Minnesota); editing *The Kerlan Awards in Children's Literature, 1975-2001* (Pogo Press); co-editing *Dear Poppa, The Berman Family WWII Letters* (Minnesota Historical Society), Ruth Plumly Thompson's *Sissajig and other surprises* (International Wizard of Oz Club) and Thompson's *The Perhappsy Chaps* (Pumpernickel Press); translating Isabelle Leveque's *The Invisible Prince/ The Prince of the Aquamarines* (Aqueduct Press), Charles Nodier's *The Crumb Fairy and other tales* (Black Coat Press), and Charles Deulin's *Tales of a Beer Drinker/Tales of King Cambrinus* (Black Coat Press); as well as stories and poems in many general, literary, and sf/fantasy magazines and anthologies, and articles on fantasy in scholarly and sf/ fantasy magazines. She won the Science Fiction Poetry Association's Rhysling Award for best short sf poem in 2004 for 'Potherb Garden.'

She was conceived in San Antonio and born in Louisville, and had a few months in St. Petersburg before Poppa was sent overseas and the the family returned to Minneapolis (where he rejoined them when the war ended), but otherwise has mostly been a long-term Minneapolis resident.

Readers can find more information at:
https://ruthberman.com

www.ingramcontent.com/pod-product-compliance
Lightning Source LLC
Chambersburg PA
CBHW060426260626
47161CB00005B/1800